PRAISE FOR

The BONE SPARROW

'A contender for the children's book of the year ... a heartrending tale about how our stories make us, and also an angry polemic, vividly convincing in is detailed description of what it means for your home to be a tent in the dust behind a guarded fence' – *THE SUNDAY TIMES*

'Outstanding ... This is an important, heartbreaking book with frequent, unexpected humour, that everyone, whether teenager or adult, should read' – *GUARDIAN*

'The story of Subhi, sensitively told and immensely moving, gives us a glimpse of what a homeless, imprisoned existence life feels like ... and how the hope invested in a vision of a better future can end up being the difference between making it out, and surrendering to despair' – *THE BIG ISSUE*

'This is a tragic, beautifully crafted and wonderful book whose chirpy, stoic hero shames us all. I urge you to read it'
THE INDEPENDENT

'... a special book' – *MORRIS GLEITZMAN, author of the acclaimed ONCE series*

'THE BONE SPARROW is one of those rare, special books that will break your heart with its honesty and beauty, but is ultimately ho ... *T*

'A profoundly poignant novel about what it means to live as a refugee' – *METRO*

'Zana Fraillon's powerful and poetic tale of friendship in the face of injustice will fly away with your heart'
KATHARINE MARSH, EDGAR AWARD-WINNING author of THE NIGHT TOURIST

'Moving and memorable, THE BONE SPARROW deserves to be read by all who care about our common humanity'
SF SAID, judge of the GUARDIAN CHILDREN'S FICTION PRIZE

'The writing is beautiful and the message of survival and bravery a universal one' – *THE BOOKSELLER*

'What a powerful story. Detention camps are no place for children. No place for humans' – *CLARE HALL-CRAGGS, BOOKTRUST*

'Think of it as a powerful polemic, yes, but also think of it as a story of the redeeming power of friendship and the vital nature of storytelling' – *THE BOOKBAG BLOG*

'This book made me cry in Temple Gardens at page 21. Loving it' – *GRASS FOR DINNER BLOG*

'So beautiful. And so important ... encourages empathy. For kids and adults alike!' – *THE BOOK ADDICT BLOG*

The Bone Sparrow

Zana Fraillon

Orion
Children's Books

ORION CHILDREN'S BOOKS

First published in Great Britain in 2016 by
Hodder and Stoughton
This paperback edition first published in Great Britain in 2017
by Hodder and Stoughton

3 5 7 9 10 8 6 4

A CIP catalogue record for this book
is available from the British Library.

ISBN 978 1 5101 0155 5

Typeset by Input Data Services Ltd, Bridgwater, Somerset

Printed and bound in Great Britain by CPI Group (UK) Ltd,
Croydon, CR0 4YY

The paper and board used in this book are from well-managed forests and other responsible sources.

FSC www.fsc.org MIX Paper from responsible sources FSC® C104740

Orion Children's Books
An imprint of
Hachette Children's Group
Part of Hodder and Stoughton
Carmelite House
50 Victoria Embankment
London EC4Y 0DZ
An Hachette UK Company

www.hachette.co.uk
www.hachettechildrens.co.uk

To those who refuse to be blinded by the glare or deafened by the hush, who are brave enough to question, and curious enough to explore. To those who will not forget. You will make a difference. And to the rest of us, so that we may learn how.

The knife worked at the bone.
Twisting, curving, smoothing.
And when the bird emerged, knowing and strong, the hand placed a coin deep into its core. 'May you for ever bring us luck and protection, and may you carry our souls to freedom.'

1

Sometimes, at night, the dirt outside turns into a beautiful ocean. As red as the sun and as deep as the sky.

I lie on my bed, Queeny's feet pushing against my cheek, and listen to the waves lapping at the tent. Queeny says I'm stupid, saying that kind of stuff. But it's true. She just doesn't see it, is all. Our maá says there are some people in this world who can see all the hidden bits and pieces of the universe blown in on the north wind and scattered about in the shadows. Queeny, she never tries to look in the shadows. She doesn't even squint.

Maá sees, though. She can hear the ocean outside too. 'You hear it, *né*?' I whisper, my fingers feeling for her smile in the dark.

In the morning, the ground still wet and foamy from where those waves washed up, I sit and trace the hundreds of animals that have swum all the way up to the tent, their faces pushing against the flaps, trying to get a look at us inside on our beds. Queeny says they aren't real beds, but just old army cots and even older army blankets. Queeny says that a real bed is made with springs and cushions and feathers, and that real blankets don't itch.

I don't think those animals would know the difference or really care much either.

This morning I found a shell washed up right along with those animals. I breathed in its smell. All hot and salty fish, like the very bottom of the ocean. And even though Queeny doesn't believe, and grunted about when was I ever going to grow up and could I please quit bothering her all the goddamn time, she still gave me her last bit of paper and said I could borrow her pen so I could write the words in black at the top of the page. *The Night Sea With Creatures.* I drew a picture as best I could with no colours and paper that curled from the damp. Using her pen and paper only cost me my soap, and I'll steal that back from her later anyway. Sisters shouldn't charge their own brothers for paper.

I snug up with Maá, my legs curled up in hers – but careful not to wake her because today is one of her tired days – and look through all the pictures in my box. I'll need to find a new box soon. The rats have eaten most of one side, and what's left is wet and mouldy, even after I left it out in the sun to dry. There are some pictures down the bottom that are headed with Maá's writing from way back, before I could write on my own. I like Maá's writing more. When she writes, it's like the words seep out on to the page already perfect. I push my fingers over Maá's letters, breathing them in like the smells from my shell.

Tomorrow, when she's better, I'll show Maá my new picture, and the shell, and tell her again about the Night Sea and its treasures. I'll tell her every little bit and listen to her laugh and watch her smile.

When I untangle my legs and whisper that it's just about breakfast time and does she want to come eat, I see her eyes open a bit and the smile start on her lips. 'Just little longer, *né*?' she says, in her English that never sounds right. 'I not hungry much, Subhi, love.'

Maá's never hungry much. The last time she ate a full meal and didn't just peck at her food was when I was only nineteen fence diamonds high. I remember because that was on Queeny's birthday and Maá always measures us on our birthdays. By now I am at least twenty-one or twenty-two, or maybe even twenty-two and a half high. I haven't been measured in a while.

Maá's never hungry much, but I'm always hungry. Eli, he reckons I must be going through a growth spurt. Eli lives in Family Tent Four with some other families because his family isn't here. Eli and I used to be in the same tent, Family Tent Three, but then the Jackets made him move. They do that sometimes. But there are forty-seven people in Family Four, and only forty-two in Family Three, so I don't know why they did. And it doesn't matter that Eli's older than me by more than Queeny is; he's my best friend and we tell each other everything there ever is to tell. Eli says we're more than best friends. We're brothers.

Eli's probably right about that growth spurt because today, after Eli and I have got our lunch, I'm still hungry even though I was given an extra big scoop in my bowl. 'You need to be strong to look after your mother, yes?'

the man serving us said. I nodded because I wanted the extra scoop, but I don't know what looking after he was talking about.

Eli leaned over and said, 'If you want to be strong, the last thing you should eat is this food.' But my mouth was already watering just looking at that bowl. We've had food shortages for the last four days and have only been getting half scoops, so there was no way Eli was going to put me off.

When I finish my lunch, I look down the rest of the long table at the others scrunched over their bowls, and the standing eaters by the wall, but no one looks like they might want to give up their food, not even after someone pulls what looks like a bit of plastic from their mouth. They just spoon through their mush more carefully.

Maá tells me never to look too closely at the food, and whenever I find flies or worms, she says I'm extra lucky because they give me protein. Once I even found a human tooth in my rice. 'Hey, Maá, is this lucky too?' I asked, and Maá looked at it and said, 'If you needing tooth.' She laughed a long time at her own joke. Longer than it was really worth, in my opinion.

Eli sees me looking and slides his half-full bowl over. 'You crazy, boy. No normal person could want more of this crap.' He says it extra loud too, and the Jackets watching take a step nearer, their hands on their sticks, just in case we didn't know already what happens if we cause a fuss in the Food Tent.

'But we're lucky, Subh, because today's food is only twelve days past its use-by date.' Eli points to the empty tubs over by the kitchen, his voice even louder. The food in my stomach starts to churn as I watch those Jackets eye each other, waiting on a signal that Eli's gone too far.

'What's your guess, then?' I ask back.

Eli must have heard my voice wobble, just that bit, because he stops staring at the Jackets and turns to me instead. 'Dog,' he whispers. 'Definitely dog.'

It's a game Eli taught me. 'Guess the Food.' Mostly the food is brown and mushed and just about impossible to guess. And none of it looks at all like the food in the magazines that sometimes show up in the Rec Room.

I eat the last spoonful from Eli's plate and close my eyes. 'Nah. It's chicken covered in chocolate sauce with a drop of honey. Dog doesn't come in tubs with use-by dates.'

Eli starts to laugh hard and his hand thumps on the table, making the bowl crash to the floor, the metal clanging so that everyone else in the room goes quiet. There isn't any questioning what those Jackets will do now, and Eli and I race out of there, jumping over the bench seats and pushing past the line of people waiting outside. We're still laughing, even though the breath is catching in our throats from our puffing, and I reckon if I don't stop soon I might spew up my lunch, and then I'll be hungry all over again.

When we've gone far enough that the Jackets won't bother following, I pull out my shell and show it to Eli. Eli, he's the only one I show all my treasures to.

'Ba sent me another,' I say.

Eli looks at me with one eyebrow raised. I don't think he's at all sure that it is my ba sending me those treasures while everyone else sleeps. But if anyone could work out how to whisper up the Night Sea to send a message to the kid he's never met, it would be my ba.

'Your dad sure as hell needs to work on his messages, because so far not a one of us can make out a word of what he's trying to say,' Eli says and slaps at the mosquito bite on his leg, all red and full of pus. I can tell just from looking the ache it must be giving him.

He has a point. But my Night Sea has been washing up treasures for five seasons now, and the first treasure I found made my maá smile deeper than ever, and her smile stayed all through that whole day. She held the treasure tight and whispered my ba's name, and wouldn't give it back until I told her she'd had long enough with it, and fair was fair. That treasure was a small statue of a knight. There are others too. The little blue car with doors that open, an old green coin with black around its edge, a star fallen all the way from space, a pen that doesn't work but feels heavy and strong in my hand, and a picture, drawn in black, of a thousand birds flying free on the wind. Every one of those treasures washed up here on a tide that no one but me sees.

I give Eli my shell and he smiles, turning it over and over in his hands. 'Nice one.' Then he sits down in the dirt and pushes it up to his ear, so hard and close that I can see the mark on his cheek, turning all red from where he has it pressed.

'Are you listening to the sound of the sea?' I ask.

'I'm listening to the stories of the sea. Do you want me to tell you what I hear?'

And now there are at least ten other kids, all gathered round, listening to Eli tell.

'A long way back, when the world was nothing but sea, there lived a whale. The biggest, hugest whale in the ocean. The whale was as old as the universe and as big as this whole country. Every night, the whale would rise to the surface and sing his song to the moon. One night . . .'

And all of us sit, Eli's story wriggling its way so deep into our brains that it can't ever fall out.

Later, I let Queeny have a listen to my shell. 'What am I listening to?' she says, the bored all over her face from my telling. 'The only thing I can hear is air swishing about.'

'That's the sound of the sea,' I tell her.

She just looks back at me. 'Pft. The sea sounds nothing like that.'

And when I show Maá, she takes the shell and listens

too. She listens for a long time, and that ache in her eyes gets even louder than ever before. She doesn't say anything, but I can tell from her face that she hears something. 'Later, *né*?' she says, her voice all low and soft like just thinking is too hard. That's how she talks mostly now.

I hide my shell, along with all the other treasures the Night Sea has washed up, down under Maá's spare shirt and trousers, where no one else will look. But just before I do, I put the shell to my ear and listen again, real hard. I'm pretty sure I can hear just the whisper of my ba's voice in there. Calling out to me. Telling me he's on his way. Telling me that it's not much longer now, because it's already been nine whole years and that's a long time to wait for a ba to come on by. *Someday*, it whispers. And the sound of the whisper is as brilliant as a thousand stars being born.

I don't tell anyone I heard him, though. Not even Eli.

2

As soon as I wake, I know today is going to be a killer. Already the air feels thick and heavy to breathe. It's going to be one of those days when the sun burns down at you from the sky and up at you from the ground, and there's not much anyone can do to get even a bit cool.

I can feel that thirst starting, so that my tongue feels big and dry. The Jackets have told us that provisions aren't due until tomorrow, and knowing that I've only got one bottle of water left, which is more empty than full, just makes me thirst even more. I look at the mould growing shapes next to my bed and try not to think about the heat. I can make out the shape of a dog with pointy ears and sharp fangs, and a truck, and over next to Maá's bed I reckon I can make out a flock of birds if I squint just a bit.

Already Queeny is cranky, standing in front of the fan and scratching at her leg rash, and going on about the heat, which no one can do a thing about and which isn't made any better by her grunting about it. But I guess no one likes the heat, because soon enough the whole tent is grumping and trying to budge in front of the fan.

I hate days like this. Days like this only get worse.

Days like this get my skin creeping and everything feels too jangly and loud and scratchy. And now my skin is creeping for real, so I start up adding numbers in my head, letting them wash around in my brain like when Maá used to sing me *tarana* songs to stop the nightmares. I keep on adding until the numbers are so big and my brain is so mixed up with getting the adding right that the whole rest of the world quietens down just that little bit.

Then Queeny comes up and jabs at me with her toe. 'Out of the way, Butt Face.' And everything is janglier and louder and scratchier than it even was before.

My legs move before I start something I don't want to start, and I'm off and out of that tent before she can make my skin even creepier. At least outside in the heat I can get away from Queeny and all the rest of the grumping.

It's only breakfast time, but already the sun looks angry. The sharpened wire on top of the fences sends splinters of light into my eyes so there's nowhere I can look without being blinded, and I can feel that grumpiness start to itch at me, no matter how tightly I squeeze my eyes or how many numbers I try to add.

I've got up to 1,289 when I hear the horn. It's Harvey's horn, because no one else honks like that. 'Queeny complaining already, hey, kid?' Harvey calls through the fence. And even though the sun is too glarey to see right, I can hear him smiling at me, right through the sun. Just like that, the grumping itch steams from my head into the sky like it wasn't ever there to begin with.

Harvey, he's one of the Jackets. Most Jackets don't bother with us Limbo kids, except to search us over with their beeper wands or shove us out of the way. But not Harvey. All the kids like Harvey. Some of the other Jackets can be nice enough too, but not like Harvey. Usually the nice ones don't stay too long anyway. But Harvey's been here longer than me, even.

The first thing Harvey does when new kids arrive is to learn their names so that he can talk with us for real, instead of talking to us by our numbers. Most people have their Boat ID as their number. Maá is NAP-24 and Queeny is NAP-23. But I was born in here, so I have a different ID. DAR-1, that's me. The 1 is because I was the first baby ever born here. But Harvey, he won't use those numbers, not even when he's supposed to.

Harvey doesn't start until lunch, but he's come in extra early today, and he tells me to wait and watch because he's brought something that he's sure I'll appreciate. I know already what it is, because Harvey, he brings this same thing every time it gets this hot.

It's a plastic pool. It's small but round, and shaped like a giant clam shell, so he always has trouble getting it through the fences and gates. While he struggles with all the locks and holding on to that pool and his bag, the other Jackets smile and laugh and jingle their keys up and down on their chains, and not a single one helps with the locks so that Harvey can get in more quickly.

'You lot aren't worth spit,' I tell them. Just not loud enough for anyone to hear. Eli says that a lot. But Eli goes right up to the person he's talking to and makes sure they hear every word.

'I've got a joke for you, kid. You ready?' Harvey says to me as soon as he gets through. Harvey always has a joke. 'What do you get if you cross a chicken with a wolf?'

'What?'

'Just the wolf. The chicken didn't stand a chance.'

It's not even funny. I tell him so, but Harvey is too busy laughing.

He puts the pool down on the ground, and even without shade to keep it cool, my toes still get excited just thinking about that water.

'It's a hose day today,' Harvey says. 'I don't care what anyone says. When it gets up to 48 degrees, I'm using the hose to fill this damn thing up to the top.'

The other Jackets don't like Harvey bringing in that pool. They say it wastes water. The last time Harvey filled it up with the hose, the water went off and didn't come back on until the truck came back three days later, so Harvey had to reckon they were probably right.

I ask Harvey about the water running out, but he just shrugs and says, 'Too late now, Subhi, it's already half full. What's up? You don't want a swim?'

I don't say that I like toilets that can flush more, or that tomorrow is my shower day and you can't have a shower without water. I don't say, because my skin is aching, waiting to jump in that cool. And hearing that water makes me thirst even worse than before, especially knowing I can't sneak even a drop because the tank water makes you sick.

But Harvey thinks of everything, and seeing my look he points to his bag, full to the top with water bottles. Harvey's great like that. I make sure not to drink too much so there's enough to go around.

Out of nowhere, kids come running to the sound of the water splashing into the pool. By the time it's full, there's already fourteen of us trying to push in quick before the water warms up as hot as the dirt, our feet fighting for space in that cool, and sloshing water up and over the side, turning the ground to mud. Even Queeny is here, splashing some of the cool up onto her face. I try to help her, but all I get is a punch on the arm for my troubles.

'Here you go, kids. Your very own sea. Don't go in too deep now.' Harvey points the hose to the sky so the last bit of water rains down on us and tingles our skin.

I've seen pictures of the sea in some of the books and magazines that come through the Rec Room. In the pictures, the sun is never angry, but warm and soft, glinting the water. Queeny says that when you swim deep down under the sea, you can watch all the fish and turtles and rays and sea flowers as bright as bright, and that you can lie on your back and let the sea carry you and you don't sink, not even a bit. The sea just lifts you up.

Some days, if the wind blows just right, I can catch a whiff of the real sea. Then, if I close my eyes and rub out everyone else pushing around me, and put all my thinking on to that water bumping against my toes, then for a second I'm there, with the sea pushing in and out against me, and going on for ever and ever, and me breathing in the wind, right down inside, and just waiting to let that water tingle over my whole body all at once and not just in drops.

Anyway, there's no wind today. Just hot.

Harvey goes to his bag and pulls out toys for the pool. Some cups with holes in the bottom that pattern down water on to the dirt, some toy plastic boats, and a water wheel for the little ones.

And a rubber duck.

Harvey throws the duck into the water, which is already red from the dirt and getting warmer by the second. The duck doesn't seem to mind, even though feet keep stomping it under the water and kicking it about. That duck just keeps bobbing back up, smiling a little duck smile all the while.

I know a bit about ducks. Harvey taught me. I know that the feathers close to the duck's skin stay dry, even when they dive as deep down underwater as they can go. I know that there aren't any nerves in a duck's feet, so that their feet don't ever get cold. I know that a male duck is called a drake, and that there are some ducks quacking around who have been alive longer than me.

Ducks can live up to twelve years, which is pretty good if you think about it.

I even know a duck joke. What grows down as it grows up? I guess that's more of a riddle than a joke.

The rubber duck Harvey put in the pool has black hair and a moustache and a tiny triangly beard. It's wearing a blue jacket and under its wing is a bit of paper with writing on it that says *To quack or not to quack.*

'What's with the duck?' Queeny says, picking it up and looking at it with that hard on her face, like she's trying to work something out.

'It's a Shakespeare duck,' Harvey smiles. I think he thinks that's funny, but neither of us gets why. 'He wrote plays – he's famous.'

Queeny stares at Harvey with the same look on her face that she used on the duck and Harvey stops talking. 'The water's already too hot. I don't know why you bother.' Queeny throws the duck so it squeaks when it hits me on the head, and is gone before I can even ask her what a play is.

I look at the duck. For a second I think it gives me a little duck nod and a wink. 'Well, hello there,' it says.

'What's a play, Harvey?'

But Harvey's not listening. He's moved over to the oldies on the plastic chairs that get all hot and sticky from being left in the sun, so whenever the oldies move, their legs sound like the Velcro on the tents. Harvey tells them to get inside. Tells them about the sun being burning today and there being no sunscreen to stop it turning their skin to sandpaper. They aren't paying him any mind, though. They just keep swatting the air like Harvey is one of the big flies that settle in your eyes and ears and won't leave you alone. They pretend they don't understand a word of what he says even though some of their English is as good as Harvey's. And when that Shakespeare duck decides he doesn't like living with Harvey so much and suggests he could come live with me instead, I know Harvey won't even notice.

The pool isn't great for properly cooling off, with so many of us squashing to get wet. Really it's only our feet that get all the way in, and then the little ones push and grump until we step out of their way. But just having that water to swish your hands through, or splash over your back and head, cools everything down just enough so your brain can think right again.

I wait a long time, until just before lunch when everyone else has got out, still complaining of the hot, and then I stick my head all the way in and under the water. It doesn't matter that there aren't any fish or turtles or rays or sea flowers as bright as bright, or that the water is hot and full of dirt, it's still brilliant.

When I stick my head under the water, the whole world stops. The earth stops spinning, the wind stops blowing, the birds in the trees freeze, and the birds that are flying fall like stones to the ground. I call out a warning first, just so they know what is coming and can get to a branch quickly.

Under the water everything is so quiet and still, and my brain stops right along with the rest of the world. I hold my breath for as long as I can and try not to feel too guilty about those birds that couldn't find somewhere to land in time.

I guess it's because of me going under the water that it happens. I guess those birds had had enough. Because when I get back to Family Three, there it is, waiting for me. And even though there's a whole bunch of us kids in there, not a single one makes a noise. All of us stop, as still as the world when I'm under water, and all of us look at my bed.

A sparrow. As sure as sure. Sitting right at the top of the bed where my head goes, so I know for sure it is talking to me and not Queeny. Not even a little bit bothered by all us kids staring at it.

That sparrow looks at me. It looks at me and I feel my mouth go as dry as before I had that drink from one of Harvey's water bottles, and hot crawls up my body so I'm suddenly sweating all over. It whistles. A single chirp. Then it flies over my head and right on out of the tent.

After, when everyone else has quietened and got on with their own doings, Queeny tells me, 'You know what that means, right? A sparrow in the house?'

I shake my head, not wanting to know what Queeny

is about to say, because Queeny, she isn't even messing.

She pulls me right in close, hugging me like she hasn't done since I was little, and just her doing that makes me more scared than ever. Her whisper in my ear cuts right through the hot of the day. 'Subhi, a sparrow in the house, that's a sign of death.'

3

Jimmie doesn't want to wake up. She knows what day it is. The house has been getting heavier and darker, preparing itself for today. Now today is here, and Jimmie doesn't want a bar of it. She pulls herself under the yellow blanket covered in monkeys that her mum gave her four years ago when she was six, and tells her brain to stop, to go back to sleep. But her brain doesn't listen. It rarely does.

Jimmie wonders if she closed herself up in a cupboard or hid herself under the bed, if she just sat in the dark all day, then maybe it would be like today didn't exist. Then she could wake up when it was tomorrow. And there would be a whole year before they had to go through this again.

Jimmie stays very still, her breath held, her heartbeat slowing. She listens. There is no noise, as if the house is holding its breath too. There are no sounds of coffee being made, or the shuffle of a newspaper being opened. No milk being slurped straight from the bottle or footsteps stomping to the bathroom. No water clanking through the pipes. Even Raticus is silent in his cage.

Outside the day has already started. People are laughing and walking and yelling and driving and working and flying in aeroplanes and swimming in the sea and growing and cooking and reading and doing. People are living, without any of them knowing what today is. None of them know that, in this house, everything has stopped. In this house, there is nothing.

The first year was the hardest. The sadness was still open and bleeding. The second year wasn't much better. Jimmie's dad told her it would get easier. And it has. Most days it has. Most days Jimmie can go the whole day without feeling that thirsting inside. But there is a lump, and a heaviness that never goes away.

Today is the beginning of the fourth year. Today, it has been three years since Jimmie last heard her mum whisper her name. Three years since every part of her life changed. Three years since her mum placed the Bone Sparrow around Jimmie's neck, her fingers shaking at the knot. '*It's your turn now, love*,' she whispered, and Jimmie closed her eyes. The next morning, her mum was dead.

At the funeral, Jimmie held on to the necklace, the sweat from her hand sinking into the bone. Her fingers worked at the Bone Sparrow the whole way through the speeches, her thumb rubbing at its smoothed back where her mum's fingers used to rub, until there was a dent in her hand the size of the sparrow and a pain at the back of her neck from the pulling.

Jimmie didn't listen to any of the words people were saying. Instead she thought of the afternoons she'd spent with her mum, just the two of them, together, before the others got home. For a moment, she thought she could feel the warmth of her mum's hands on her shoulders and the slightest pressure of a kiss placed gently on her head. Sitting in between Jonah and her dad, feeling them close, she could almost imagine that nothing had changed. That her mum would pop through that door any second. '*What a mix-up! Wait till you hear what happened!*'

In those first weeks after the funeral, Jimmie helped her dad pack up her mum's clothes. They put them into boxes and her dad pushed them high up into the attic. They did the same with her mum's things – her books, her pictures, her jewellery, everything – sweeping them into boxes so they wouldn't make her dad weep and cry and curl into a ball on the floor.

All through that clearing, Jimmie had kept the Bone Sparrow necklace tucked under her shirt. She didn't want to remind her dad that she wore it now. She didn't want him to cry again.

It was while they were packing up the bedroom that Jimmie found the notebook. Small and broken and full of words she couldn't read. She wanted to ask her dad or Jonah to read the words to her, but she knew she couldn't. It didn't matter anyway. Her mum had written down each and every word in that book, and one day Jimmie would read them and hear her mum's voice again. So she didn't pack the book into the boxes with the other things.

That was three years ago. She still can't read the words. Still can't hear her mum's voice.

Outside in the garden, she hears a howl, long and pained. Her dad is awake. Even through blocked ears Jimmie can hear him crying. She holds the Bone Sparrow above her head, watching the bird spin lazy circles in the air, its wings spread wide and the white of the bone blossoming into green around the middle where a coin used to sit. Her mum told her about the Bone Sparrow when she was little. Told her how it had protected her family for generations. Told her how it carried the souls of all her family, keeping them together and safe on their journey.

But Jimmie doesn't feel protected. She doesn't feel safe. All she feels is that lump, and that heaviness, that never go away.

4

I tell Eli about the sparrow. About what Queeny said. Eli starts up laughing like it's the biggest joke I've ever told. He says that a tent is a tent and a house is a house and there's no need to confuse the two, so I have nothing to get so worked up about.

But that tent is all the house I've ever known, so I don't know if Eli is right about that one.

I tell the Shakespeare duck that I rescued from Harvey, and he looks me up and down with his little duck eyes and says that clearly I'm done for and could I please arrange for someone nice to take him when I'm dead. I tell him that if I'm going to die, I'm sure as hell taking him with me, and there isn't anyone else in this camp who would take the time to talk to a rubber duck. He doesn't say much after that.

I tell Harvey too, but he just wants to know what I've gone and left in my bed to attract the birds, and that we already have enough problems with the rats without me attracting the birds as well.

I don't tell Maá, in case it worries her. In case she thinks it's true.

And now it's like those damn sparrows are everywhere. Watching me. Maybe they've been there all along, but ever since that one sat staring at me from the top of my bed, I can't stop seeing them.

Eli and I are walking the fences, and when I bend down to tie my shoe, there's another sparrow, hopping right in front of me, and looking at me with its head turned to the side. 'It's another one, Eli, look!'

Eli throws his hands in the air. 'If you mention that stupid bird one more time then I'll kill you myself to get it over with.' He can't say it without smiling, though. 'Now, if you want to keep those shoes of yours, you'd better start earning them. Come on, Squirt, we have work to do.'

There are only fourteen pairs of real shoes in this whole entire camp, even though there must be near about nine hundred pairs of feet. And one of those pairs of shoes belongs to me. My shoes are blue with white laces and some black bits on the side. They were more than big enough when I first got them and I still have to stuff paper in them to stop them from falling off with each step. I'm growing into them, though. Eli taught me to tie my laces, which is something, because even Queeny can't tie laces. If she ever gets proper shoes, Queeny will have to come to me, begging for me to teach her how.

Eli got me my shoes. He said I needed them if I was going to run packages with him. Package delivery is Eli's business. At first, I didn't want to run. Not a bit. But then I saw the happy on people's faces when Eli delivered. And I saw the shoes. I gave him my too-small flip-flops that very day, and he gave me the shoes, and now I can walk anywhere I want without stones poking up through the soles and the hot eating at my feet.

Eli calls us partners, and together we trade most of

what people want for most of what we've got. People just tell us what they need and what they are going to swap to get it. A shirt for flip-flops, or soap for toothpaste – whatever they want. Eli keeps a stash hidden away and most mornings we run a couple of packages and keep people happy.

When the Jackets hand out provisions from the truck, we don't get to choose. You get what you get and you don't get upset, that's what Harvey says. The other Jackets you don't even bother complaining to, even if they've run out of mosquito sticks by the time you get to the front of the line, or if they give you only one bottle of water for each day instead of two like you're supposed to get. Complaining only gets your one bottle of water tipped into the dirt or the rest of your supply put back in the truck. So people come to me and Eli instead. Eli, he keeps all those orders and all those swaps stuck in his head so no one can find a written-down list and get us in trouble.

Every so often Eli gets something for us as well, and we don't have to trade a single thing. He said that's our pay for taking the risk of running the packages all over the camp in the first place. We get toothpaste, because Eli reckons having good teeth is important, and I get Maá extra water when I can, and pads for when she and Queeny have their women's time so they don't have to ask the Jackets whenever they need to use the toilet. Once Eli even gave me a whole box of toilet paper so that we could use more than the maximum six small squares that the Jackets give you. I have trousers that fit right without a rubber band to hold them up, and four pairs of underwear, which is twice as many as is allowed. And my shoes.

Eli and me, we know all the squeezeways in and about the place. The places where the cameras don't see, and the flaps that are loose enough to get you into the backs of the kitchen, and the wobbly wire between the toilet blocks. That's how we get the packages all over the whole camp and not just all over Family Compound.

Sometimes you can get right up close to the fences to pass the package through. Like if you're delivering to Ford Compound, which is the place you get put if you need to be kept more safe than usual because someone keeps on hurting you, or if your brain gets so mushed from being here that you keep on hurting yourself. We can also pass straight through to Alpha Compound, which is where all the grown men without families live. Family is right in the middle between Ford and Alpha so our fences edge theirs. Then there's Hard Road behind us and separating us from the other compounds on the other side. Hard Road isn't really a road, but we call it that because that's where all the hard buildings are. The ones made out of container blocks or bricks, like the old School Room, which isn't used any more, or the Computer Room or the toilets and showers.

But even having Hard Road right in the middle doesn't stop us. If we need to deliver to the other side, like if we're delivering to Delta, where all the new arrivals go, or Echo, which is another compound where men with no families go, then we have to make a drop behind the kitchens or reach through the wobbly wire at the back of our toilet block, where it edges up to the back of their toilet block. That's the hardest, and sometimes if the toilets haven't been cleaned then you can end up with all sorts on your arms.

Eli has worked out how to deliver to every compound there is – all except Beta Compound. That's where the Jackets take people they reckon are trouble. There are extra fences and extra Jackets, and the fences have electricity and the Jackets have dogs. The people in there live in small containers by themselves and only get to come out for a cigarette and a walk in the morning and afternoon. Beta Compound must just about be the loneliest place on earth.

Eli has to keep changing where he keeps his stash. If the Jackets find it, then there'll be trouble for sure, especially because sometimes Eli finds a way of fingering extra things from the provisions truck. Like when he managed to steal a whole box of underwear.

'Plan B, Subhi. You always need to have a Plan B. Do you know how many orders we have for underwear? There are people here walking around with more holes than undies, and no one wanting to swap. What else could I do?' And he was right. That week we ran more packages than ever before.

This week the stash is kept at the back of the kitchens, down under where all the rubbish is dumped. As soon as we get there, the rats give us a look, knowing that we're about to disturb their lunch, and I can feel that zipping in my legs that I get every time I'm about to run a package. That kind of excited, scared zip that makes everything feel a little bit sharper and more real.

Eli sorts right through that stench down to the very bottom of the pile. I stand back, my hand over my nose to try and stop the taste of rot from getting in my mouth. Eli reaches into a bag and holds up a shirt, tied into a ball. 'This one is for Pietre, over in Alpha. He's going to give you toothpaste, which is to go to Assad in Family Two, got it?'

'Got it. Assad, Family Two.' I poke at the shirt, trying to work out what's wrapped up inside, because there is a hardness in the middle. Eli's rule is never open the packages, but there's no rule about guessing.

'Assad has a mozzie stick, which you bring back here. 'K?'

'Sure thing.'

'And, Subhi? Watch your back, little bruda.' Eli says that every time he gives me a package. He always musses my hair when he says it, too. Eli used to have a little brother for real, but he doesn't any more. He still keeps his brother's glove in his pocket, though. It's red and small and Eli says it brings him luck. I reckon he's right too, because Eli has the walk of someone who knows they have luck at their back.

I still can't work out what's in the package, even when I'm half way back to Alpha. Alpha has more cameras on the tops of its fences than we do in Family, but Eli and I found where the blind spot is – right over in the corner where the fence hits the brick wall of the shower blocks, and kind of half hidden behind a couple of bushes.

I go to the corner and give the whistle so they know there's a package coming through the fence. I can see Pietre walking up to meet me, his eyes all red and puffy from the dust sickness, and I just about think I've worked out that there's a box of cigarettes or a pack of playing cards inside this shirt when I see Pietre stop, frozen to the spot. He turns slowly, slowly, and shakes his head at me.

I know that look. I know by the way the scared covers Pietre's face. A Jacket is here.

I don't want to turn around. I can feel those eyes burning into my back. Here I was, so caught up in what was inside this damn package that I stopped watching out for who might be watching out for me. I forgot to watch my back. I hate it when I do that. When my brain wanders off and leaves me behind to pay for it.

I turn slowly, my eyes on the ground, but I can see the black boots flashing from the sun and the black trousers with the cuffs browned from the dirt, and I can tell from the sour smoke smell that it's not just any Jacket.

It's Beaver.

My chest gets all tight and I start up coughing and trying to suck in more air, and all I can think is that Queeny was right. That the sparrow was a sign of death. All I can think is, I'm about to die.

5

When I was little I had nightmares. Nightmares about people screaming, about being stuck in a dark hole, about losing Maá and Queeny, about running and never being able to run fast enough. One nightmare kept coming back. That nightmare was always about Beaver. Beaver coming and catching me. Sometimes I still have that nightmare even though I'm grown.

Eli says Beaver hates all of us because one time he almost got killed when a man in here turned crazy and grabbed a hammer. Beaver ended up losing his eye because of it, and now just has his eyelid sewn down flat over where his eye used to be. Eli reckons that's what makes him so mean.

But I reckon Beaver was always mean, and the almost-being-killed just made him meaner. Beaver's the kind of person who gives you an extra kick for not getting out of his way fast enough, or tips your maá's dinner into the dirt so she has to pick it up with her fingers and eat it fresh from the ground in front of him, all covered in grit and all.

And what Eli reckons doesn't really make sense either, because Harvey was almost killed in the same craziness, and he's as nice as ever. It was Beaver who saved Harvey. Harvey was crouched down looking at something and the man went for him from behind. Harvey never even saw it coming. But Beaver did, and he jumped in front when the man went for Harvey. I guess Beaver's meanness just picks its moments.

Or maybe it just picks its people. Eli reckons Beaver saving him is why Harvey can't ever say bad against Beaver, even though he wouldn't stand for any other Jacket treating people the way Beaver does. Eli reckons that makes Harvey spineless and not worth spit, but I kind of get it. I think.

Eli said I was never to run packages when Beaver was on. If ever something had to be delivered when Beaver was working, Eli would take it himself and keep me well out of it. I saw what happened when Eli got caught with a package. Beaver handcuffed Eli with his arms twisted behind his back and shoved him into the Jackets' offices. And after, when Eli came out of the office, he just rubbed at the red raw on his wrists and wiped the blood from his nose and told me I wasn't to ever run a package when Beaver was on. Not ever.

But I guess Beaver changed his hours without us knowing. Because here he is, looking down at me with his one eye and a smile without even a smidge of happiness in it.

Everyone in Alpha is watching, their cigarettes in their mouths and their heads shaking. I hope more than anything that this is an Inside package.

An Inside package is a package swapped between us. Stuff we all get anyway, like flip-flops or a bar of soap. But sometimes the packages have stuff from Outside. I don't know how Eli gets that stuff in here or what gets swapped in return, because I can't imagine that people on the Outside need to swap us for our soap. I don't even know what's in the Outside packages. I asked Eli once and he said it's the stuff of kings, which didn't make any more sense than my ba's messages sent on the Night Sea. Usually Eli only gives me the Inside packages. But sometimes . . .

My throat is as dry as the dirt. Eli always tells me, 'Never let anyone see your scared,' and I try as hard as I can but trying isn't doing, and I've never been handcuffed before and I've never been taken into the offices, and thinking on all of that is fouling my stomach close to spewing.

'What are you doing back there?' Beaver's voice sounds as dark as the Jackets' dogs when they don't like a person. I can't talk. I can't say a single thing. His hand is hard and scratchy, grabbing at my shirt and pulling me towards him so that my teeth clang on my tongue and I can taste blood, and my brain is buzzing louder and louder.

'I asked you a question.'

I still can't talk. He shoves me backwards so hard that my feet leave the ground and my head cracks into the bricks behind me, and for a moment all I can see are little lights flashing in and out. When I crash into the dirt, Beaver has the package. And he's opening it.

It's Queeny who saves me. Queeny, who looks as close to a superhero as I've ever seen. She swoops down to my side, her hair flying out behind her, and stands in front of me, my shield from Beaver.

Beaver opens the shirt. I see what's inside. And I feel my heart start to beat extra fast because for a while there I think it had just about stopped. It's washing powder. Safe, safe Inside washing powder. Beaver takes the washing powder and tips it into the dirt. Then he stomps the shirt into the dirt as well, and I can hear it ripping. I hope that Pietre has something else to swap because that shirt won't be much good any more.

Queeny says to me, 'I told you to go straight to do the laundry,' and says to Beaver, 'He always comes out here to play. I told him to go to the laundry to wash that shirt . . .' Queeny keeps talking and her hands keep flapping and she only stops when Beaver spits on to the dirt and some of it goes on her foot.

Then he walks away. I can feel tears snaking down my cheeks and Queeny's arm wraps around me, pulling me back to our tent. I suddenly get a feeling like when I was little and I'd wake from my nightmares. Queeny would always be right there next to me to hush me back to sleep, and even though I was scared, I'd get all warm in my belly, knowing my sister was looking after me.

I haven't felt like that in a long time.

Queeny puts me into our bed, my legs and hands still shaking, and she whispers to get some rest. To get some sleep, and that everything is all right now. She tells me to think on one of my stories and put Beaver out of my head for a bit. And even though it's still day, I can feel my brain closing and all I can do is shut my eyes.

My ba used to tell me his stories. A long time ago, before I was even born. He would huddle over Maá's stomach, me curled inside, and he'd rub his hands all over her belly and pull the heat right out of it, taking away all the pain that roared through her.

All the time Ba was pulling on that pain, he was telling me stories. Telling them right through Maá's belly so they could reach my little baby ears. The stories from a time so long gone that he couldn't know except by being told them himself. And even though I know I can't know what that was like, even though I know I can't really remember from before I was born, in my head I do. In my head I can hear my ba's voice washing up against me.

When I was little, I used to ask Maá to tell me the stories Ba whispered. She always said no, that she could never get the words just right. 'Your ba is writer. Poet. You wait when he tell right. Soon he come. Soon he whisper his poet, right to your ear. I tell my stories instead,' she'd say. 'Not so good, not so bad.' Queeny and I would scrunch up on the bed, our legs all twisted together, flopping over Maá, and we'd lie back with our eyes closed, letting those stories burn themselves into us. They were perfect. Each one.

We called them her Listen Now stories, because each

ne started with 'Listen now, Subhi. Listen ' which is Queeny's real name, but only s her that. Most of the stories were good and happy. All about their dog and their donkey in Burma, and swimming in the sea and watching shooting stars fall from the sky. Some were Rohingya stories, passed down from maás to their kids since forever back. And some weren't so happy. They were stories we had to hear, though. About being told the Rohingya don't exist. About having their house burnt down, and their animals killed. About not being allowed to go to school or to work or to the hospital. About being arrested and made to build roads and dig holes for no money. About running from the police and soldiers. Lots of running. About people disappearing and people dying. About my ba being arrested for writing his poems, and not coming back. About soldiers finding Maá and Queeny and putting them on a boat with other Rohingya. About being told if they come back to Burma they'd be killed. About coming here. About every country in the world saying we don't belong. Not in this place. Not in any place.

And then one day Maá stopped the stories. The good, happy ones as well. One day she just said, 'No more. Looking back only brings sad, Subhi. Now look forward. No more back.' That was when Maá stopped talking to me in Rohingya too. She reckons that if I only speak English, then no one will think I am any different when we get out. 'Someday, Subhi,' Maá says, 'someday they see we belong.'

I tell myself the stories as best as I can, but the words aren't right the way I remember. Not like the way Maá told them. And when I ask her again to tell me a story, she says she's too tired. She says she can't remember right, her fingers rubbing at her eyes like it's too bright to think. Someday Maá will tell me again, her mushed-up English and Rohingya words all in together. Someday I'll learn Rohingya for myself so I'll be able to talk it without even trying to think how. Someday Maá will see that looking back is just as important as looking forward, no matter how much sad it carries. Someday my ba will figure a way to get free, to get out of Burma, and then we'll all of us be together. And he will sit and tell me his own stories and his own poems for himself, just like Maá used to say he would. Then I won't ever forget. Not a bit.

But until then I keep on at Maá every night, asking her for a story. Just a single one. Because sometimes, in here, when people stop talking, and stop asking, and stop remembering, that's when they start to lose that piece of themselves. That's when their brains start to mush. It happens a lot.

Even though Maá doesn't even hear my asking any more, I keep trying, without even thinking on an answer. I keep asking every night, because if I don't . . .

But I guess I was tired. I guess after Beaver my

brain just decided it had had enough for the day. There was an ache at the back of my head that wouldn't let up and blood on my fingers from when I touched the bump where I hit the bricks. Everything in my body was screaming at me to stop. To close my eyes and stop thinking so loud. So I curled up 0n my bed and slept through dinner and curfew, and I only woke up in the middle of the night when a Jacket shone his torch in my face and made me tell him my number. DAR-1.

It is only then, when I'm trying to fall back to sleep, that I realise. For the first time, I hadn't asked Maá. I didn't ask her.

And then everything changed.

6

Jimmie likes school. She just doesn't get there much since her mum died. If Jonah doesn't get her to the bus stop on time, then there isn't much she can do because that bus only comes past once a day and there's no way Jonah's driving an hour to get her there.

Sometimes the school calls, but they only have Dad's old mobile number, the one Jonah has been using since Dad threw it against the wall and smashed the screen. And when Jonah answers, the school doesn't even ask to leave a message. It's not like Jimmie is the only one not going to school. Most times she goes, they're lucky if half the class is there, and they only go over the same stuff they've gone over the day before, anyway. It doesn't bother Jimmie. School just isn't that important.

But reading is important. Her mum loved reading. Every night they hopped into bed and Jimmie would choose from the pile of books they'd borrowed from the mobile library, and her mum would start reading. When Jimmie started school she'd thought that she would learn straight away. But it didn't work like that. Not for Jimmie. 'It just takes time, love,' her mum would say. But it was more than that. And then her mum died and nothing really seemed to matter any more.

Now, Jimmie wonders if her dad even remembers that she can't read, or maybe he just figures that the school fixed her. Like the way Jonah fixes the telly by sticking a coat hanger in the top. Yesterday her dad saw Jimmie looking through one of the books from the shelf above the telly. She liked the smell of the pages, all dusty and warm. 'Is it any good, love?' he asked her.

Jimmie didn't answer. She looked at the picture on the cover and wondered why her dad couldn't work out that it wasn't a kid's book she was sniffing. She guessed he just hadn't noticed.

Her dad never seemed to really notice much these days. Sometimes that was a good thing. Like last week when she took his bike for a spin out along the track and stacked it against a rock because she thought you had to pedal backwards to work the brakes. That was how Jimmie's old bike had done it. But she'd grown out of her old bike years ago. When her dad saw the wheel, all bent to the side and out of shape, he rubbed his eyes and shook his head, like he couldn't quite remember when he'd done that. Jonah smiled at Jimmie and whispered, 'I'll get you a bike for your birthday, if you like,' and Jimmie felt a buzz in her legs just thinking about it.

Before coming here, Jimmie's family had moved around a lot. Jimmie couldn't remember how many times they had stuffed everything they owned into their trailer and gone. She couldn't remember how many schools she'd started at, or how many friends she'd made, just to up and leave without so much as a goodbye. When they found this place, though, Jimmie's mum said they were staying put. 'This is where we've been headed all along, kids!'

Jimmie's dad said, 'Rubbish. It's just where the work

is.' But they hadn't moved again. They'd bought an old bird bath and Jimmie helped her mum keep it full and clean. Her mum planted a lemon tree, because all houses need a lemon tree, she'd said, and as soon as the first lemons were ripe, their mum started making pancakes with lemon and sugar every Sunday for breakfast. She even started a veggie garden, filling an old bath with dirt that stank and singing to the seeds until they all pushed their way up towards her voice.

When she died, Jimmie and Jonah and Dad had planted a wattle out the front because wattles were Mum's favourite tree in the whole world. That was when Jimmie knew they wouldn't leave again. They couldn't. Even when Jimmie's dad lost his job along with the rest of the town, and had to find a new job working shifts, which took him away from home for days at a time. This is where their mum had been happiest. And so they would stay. Because this is where their mum was. No one else would want to move into an empty town full of nothing but memories, anyway.

But Jimmie likes exploring the memories. When Jimmie wanders, her thoughts stop buzzing, and the ache at the back of her head disappears. She takes her pet rat, Raticus, with her, snug in her pocket or perched on her shoulder, hidden under her hair. It's nice knowing she's exploring with someone. She likes imagining who else walked where she is walking, or who else touched this exact spot. She likes imagining what they would have been thinking when they sat on this rock or climbed this tree or looked at this creek. She likes imagining what their lives are like. She likes imagining that some part of that person is still here, just a shadow of them, and that if she concentrates hard enough, then she could almost be that person. Just for a moment. Jimmie explores a lot.

She explores the houses left to rot when the mines closed and everyone lost their jobs. There's loads of stuff to find in those houses. Forgotten things hidden under fallen roof plaster or kicked under mouldy carpet. Once Jimmie even found a pair of socks with ten twenty-dollar bills rolled up inside. Her dad said he would have to hand them in to the cop station on his way to work, but then Jimmie found the socks tucked into his drawer.

She explores the road that winds its way out of town, past the bus stop that has only two times on the timetable, and eventually reaches the water. Some days, Jimmie bundles Raticus into her pocket and throws off most of her clothes and goes swimming, ignoring the *EXTREME DANGER – ACHTUNG! CROCODILES INHABIT THESE WATERS. ATTACKS CAUSE INJURY OR DEATH* sign that sticks out from the bank. Jonah has read that sign to her often enough for Jimmie to know it off by heart. She just figures there isn't enough meat on her to satisfy a hungry croc. Anyway, not many people come fishing around here any more, and everyone knows that the crocs follow the fishermen.

She explores further up the hill, leaving her house behind her, wandering all the way to the edge of town, where the windows of the shops are boarded up or broken. The last shop to shut was the milk bar. Now it's a fifty-minute drive to get a bottle of milk, meaning that more often than not Jimmie eats her cereal with water, or doesn't bother with breakfast at all.

There's only one place Jimmie hasn't explored. Down the hill. Down near the Centre. Jonah and Jimmie had headed down there once, but stopped. There was a feeling down there. A sort of sadness in the air, and they'd both turned back without saying a thing about it.

And then today at school, some of the kids had been talking. Saying how lucky those people were in the Centre. How they had everything. Good clothes and thousands of toys and books and computers and teachers and doctors who lived right there in the Centre so you didn't have to drive for two days if you were sick. And one of the boys, Max, he said he saw a container get delivered to the Centre, and inside it was full of brand-new bikes. Only a few kids at Jimmie's school had a bike. The school used to have a couple for the kids to use, but they had disappeared just about as soon as they'd come.

'Are you sure about that container?' Jimmie had asked, and Max had spat in his hand to double promise.

But Jimmie remembered her mum and dad talking about the Centre when they first moved in. '*It's not right*,' her mum had said, and Jimmie's ears had pricked up. '*That's no way to treat people.*' Remembering that, Jimmie couldn't make sense of what Max was saying. It hadn't sounded like the kind of place that would give out bikes. Maybe things had changed. Or maybe Max was just wrong.

Now, lying in bed, the Centre is all Jimmie can think about. Outside the wind has picked up, so it almost sounds as though waves are crashing against the dirt outside their house. The wind has never sounded like that before. And suddenly Jimmie needs to know. She needs to see what's down there. So she grabs her mum's book and her backpack and tiptoes down the stairs and climbs out the bathroom window, avoiding the creaking door so she doesn't wake her dad, and starts down the hill. Past the gum tree that she climbs almost every day, past the rock where she once found a red-bellied black snake, past the termite mound that is taller than Jimmie is, and all the way to the bottom of the hill.

It's then that she finds the fence.

It was Jonah who taught Jimmie to explore. Nothing could ever stop them. Especially not a fence. 'A fence just means there's something interesting inside,' Jonah used to say.

And just because this fence has lights and cameras, and rolls and rolls of razor wire on top, that doesn't mean she can't get through. That just makes it more of a challenge. Jonah taught Jimmie how every fence has a weak spot – it's only a matter of finding it.

Jimmie sits in the dirt for a long time, watching the fence and the light and the shadows and the cameras, and then she moves towards the fence. She just has to find its weak spot, is all.

7

I can't sleep. All that sleep has been sucked right out of me. Now my brain is buzzing in and out, remembering what happened. Remembering Beaver. Remembering that I didn't ask for a story. I have to ask for a story. Every night. That's the rule. There are some rules that no one has to say. There are some rules you just know.

But I didn't ask. I want to wake Maá, to ask her, to say the words so it's done and so we're safe. So she remembers to think on her stories while she sleeps. So she holds on to the good. So she remembers Ba. So she tells again how he's coming, even if she just tells it in her head, and not out loud. I can feel the panic sticking in my throat and crawling along my skin, and my brain is telling me to calm down because they're just words, and I want to wake her but I can't because then tomorrow will definitely be a tired day.

I sit up in bed and look around, but no one else is awake. I can tell by the still and heavy in the tent. The Shakespeare duck tells me he's awake, but I tell him he doesn't count because his eyes can't actually ever shut.

'Rude,' he says back, and puffs himself up.

Usually when the Jackets shine their torches around the tents, there are just as many eyes glinting back as not. After a bit the Jackets go and play cards and drink their drink and don't bother too much except to come and wake us to check our IDs if they're bored or angry or just want to mess about.

But the nights when the Night Sea comes belong just

to me. And tonight the thick quiet in the tent starts my brain wondering if maybe the Night Sea is on its way. I told Maá about this once when I was little, and she said it made sense. Maá reckoned that my Night Sea must pull everyone else's waking in on its currents and wash back deep sleep, nice and pure. Maá says it's because I listen to the earth. She says if everyone would listen to the stories deep down inside the earth, we would hear the whisperings of everything there is to hear, and if everyone did that, then just maybe we wouldn't all get stuck so much. Usually thinking on that helps me get to sleep, and then I don't know if the sea I'm hearing is the real Night Sea or just the one in my dreams.

But tonight I can already hear the water lapping at the tent's edge. And maybe, maybe the Night Sea will make it all right that I didn't ask. Maybe the Night Sea will make it OK, what happened with Beaver. Maybe the Night Sea will show me how to get Maá to wake up again properly, so we can play jacks and she can let me win, or draw memory cards or make stick gardens or tell jokes. Maybe I will get to see Eli's whale, as old as the universe and as big as a country, sing its song to the moon.

I can hear those waves now, and suddenly I want that sea to float me up, to cover me in its waves and show me everything there is to see. And right now, I need that water. I grab the duck and crawl out from under Queeny and toe over the bunks, trying not to frighten the rats scuttling about. I push through the flap as quiet as I can.

But there's no sea. Not even a puddle. Just the wind blowing the top of the dirt to swirling, like it does sometimes, and right in the middle of the swirl, right outside my tent, right in front of me, is a girl. Like that red dirt had up and whooshed her straight from the ground.

'Where's the sea?' the duck says. 'You promised me a sea.'

'I never said promise. What I said was—' And then I shake my head and shove the duck in my pocket so that girl doesn't think I'm totally bonkers talking to a rubber duck.

The girl is just standing, watching me. I rub my eyes because what they're seeing can't make sense in my brain. But the rubbing doesn't change a thing.

There she is. Just a girl, standing right there and breathing in the night air. That girl, she isn't one of us. I can tell just from looking. None of us has hair like that. Like a fire burning up from her head and frizzed straight out to the sky. None of us, excepting me and Eli, has shoes – but that girl does. She has a backpack too. And she's holding a book. A real book.

Then the girl leans down and pushes her hand deep into the dirt, like she's feeling for a heartbeat. I wonder if she listens to the earth too.

She looks at me and smiles.

Maá used to tell me about my great-great-great-ba,

from way back. He only had one foot, but he used to travel all over, healing everyone. Maá said he had a guardian angel, except the way she said it was, 'He have luck wings. But it go, same as his foot. *Ói*, Someday, Subhi, luck wings comes back. Then we all be happy and luck again.' Queeny and I would laugh and Maá would laugh too, and none of us would know for real whether we were laughing about a lost guardian angel coming all the way to the bum end of nowhere to find us, or at the way Maá talked all out of whack and tried to be serious.

But when I see that girl, my brain jumps to thinking about our guardian angel, and for a moment, a long moment, I get to thinking that maybe that girl is our guardian angel. Even though it seems kind of strange that a guardian angel would wear trousers with more holes all over than mine, even, and a shirt that is way too big, but maybe that's to hide the wings, which are a definite must for any guardian angel worth their salt.

Then that girl hocks up the biggest ball of snot I've ever seen – and I've seen some pretty big balls of snot being hocked around here – and she spits that snot right on to the ground. That's when I know. Guardian angels don't hock up snot.

That girl and I watch each other for a while, and then she shrugs. A quick shrug. Like she's been talking that whole time and has finally run out of things to say. I think she must be about to go. Her body turns away and she looks out into the dark. Then she stops. Like she's remembered.

'Do you lot have any bikes in here?'

I shake my head. I remember the stories Eli told me about his bike, which was black, and how he used to ride it to school and to his grandma's house, and that when he was riding it down a big hill it made him feel like he was riding on the wind itself. Every time he told it, I tried to imagine what it would feel like to ride the wind. But no matter how many different ways Eli told it, it never really felt real.

But maybe I haven't heard that girl right, because a bike wouldn't work in here. There are too many fences and tents in the way and not even a single hill.

'Huh,' she says, 'I knew Max was lying. So what's your name, then?'

'Subhi. What's yours?'

The girl doesn't answer.

'Is that your book?' I ask, and wish I hadn't because I know all the books in here and that isn't one of them and who else's would it be?

'Course it is. Why? Can you read?'

I nod so fast that my head starts to aching again.

'Hm,' the girl says, whispering something so soft to herself that I'm pretty sure I wasn't meant to hear it.

Then she turns and walks into the shadows, her arms banging against her legs. 'See ya,' she says, and I want to call out to her, to tell her to wait, because there is something about that girl that is like no one else I've ever met. Like no one I've ever even thought of. But no matter how hard my eyes search those shadows, it is only her voice that is left. Like she's up and turned invisible right there in front of me.

It isn't until I've been sitting there for a long time after that I hear a quacking coming from my trousers. When I pull out the Shakespeare duck, he looks at me and says, 'She didn't even tell you her name.'

8

When I wake up in the morning and think back on that girl, I wonder if maybe I dreamt her. It doesn't make any sense that a girl from Outside could get her way in here. No sense at all. Sometimes that happens. Sometimes my dreams seem so real that it takes a while for me to tell real from dream when I wake up. Like the other day when I dreamt I had already lined up for my shower and when I woke I realised I had to wait in line all over again.

But there is her hocked-up ball of snot, and there are her fingertip marks, still in the dirt. I put my hand on top. They are just about a perfect fit. I curl up next to the prints and close my eyes, letting the earth pull me deep down to its stomach and wrap me tight in all its whisperings. I don't move, not until Queeny kicks me to come have breakfast because the bell has just gone for seven o'clock and the kitchen's about to shut until lunch.

When Harvey comes along the line with his security wand to check us all over, he asks why my face is covered in dirt. I tell him I've been listening for the stories from the earth. I don't tell him about the girl.

'He was just lying there, like his brain had melted,' Queeny adds, 'and, actually, that explains a lot.'

I can't help smiling, imagining my brain melting into the dirt. I can't think of anything to say back, though. I never can. Not until it's too late.

But Harvey just scrounches down in the dirt and

wipes the red from my face, his beeper wand hanging from his wrist, not even caring at all about the others going back and forth without being checked for security.

'It's not silly at all, kid,' he says. Even though he's looking at me, I can see that he's talking more to Queeny. 'Do you know that there are seven different types of dirt? You can tell a whole lot about a place by that dirt under your feet. All about people and animals and the history of a place, just by—'

Queeny shushes him with her hand, her face bright and open. 'Seven types, hey?' For a moment, Harvey thinks she's interested. 'Do any of those types of dirt turn into a sea at night then?' She twists her mouth into a smile and rolls her eyes.

'Pfft,' the Shakespeare duck says from my pocket. 'What does she know? I bet she doesn't even know that I talk.'

Harvey and Queeny look at me then, like they can't work out why I'm laughing.

Seeing that girl all swooshed up from the dirt last night has somehow turned Beaver into a memory, with only the dried-out blood and lump grown up at the back of my head to remind me, so when Eli comes charging up, his eyes hard and dog mad, I can't even figure on what he's saying or why he's angry. Not until he says, 'If he touches you again, I'll kill him. You hear me? I'll find a way. When I see him, I'll tell him—'

But Queeny puts her hand on Eli and tells him to calm down and 'Shush up' and 'Just forget about it, will ya?'

'What happened? Who did what?' Now Harvey is on at me too. I wish they'd all just shut up about it so I can get back to thinking about the girl.

Eli looks at Harvey and his eyes are just about spitting. 'Beaver. He hit him. Threw him against a wall.' Eli grabs me and pushes my head down so Harvey can see the lump at the back. Bloody Eli is making it hurt more. My eyes are about to water and I can feel my nose start to drip, and I wish they all would just let me be. But Eli, he won't let go. He's pulled me into him now, like it was Harvey that had shoved me instead of Beaver. 'Who knows what he would have done or where he would have taken him if Queeny hadn't been watching out? But don't pretend like you care.'

Harvey turns to Eli with angry twisting his face. I want to tell Eli that Harvey does care, that I know he does, and that I'm fine, but I can't say anything. When I squeeze the duck in my pocket, he gives a little squeak to let me know he understands.

Eli sniffs and nods, like Harvey knows just what he's on about. Harvey looks me over, with his eyes darting all about my face, and then he turns and walks away.

Queeny looks at my head. 'You'd better clean that cut so it doesn't get infected and put germs all through your blood and make you die.' And now all I can think about is germs going all through my blood and making me die.

The Shakespeare duck says he reckoned he could see the germs multiplying last night already but he didn't want to say anything in case I got scared. But what does he know? He's just a stupid duck.

Eli pulls me even closer and tilts my head down to look again. 'Don't be silly. Germs can't kill you. But maybe we should go get it clean. Has your maá seen it?' And the way Eli is talking is making me think that maybe Queeny wasn't being so stupid after all. Maybe that Shakespeare duck does know what he's talking about.

Eli rests his face on my head then and breathes out, long and slow. 'I'm sorry, bud. I didn't know. I would never have let you run if I'd known . . .' He lets go of me and reaches into his pocket. 'Here. I got you something.' He pulls out three whole muesli bars, still in their wrappers and not even past their use-by.

'There are boxes of them,' he smiles. 'I heard them talking, the Jackets. They're sending them all back because of the wrappers.'

I can't see anything wrong with the wrappers. Eli points to the name of the bars – Freedom Bars. 'I guess they don't want us getting any ideas, hey?'

Queeny and Eli laugh as we leave the line and head for Eli's tent, because who needs slimy porridge full of grit when we've got muesli bars for breakfast? All the while I'm thinking that I just need to get rid of Queeny so's I can tell Eli about the girl.

But when we get to the tent, we see the Jacket.

He has a paper in his hands and Searching For Someone all across his face. Eli looks at me, and I can tell that we are both thinking the same thing. That Eli's paper has finally come through. Eli's been waiting a long time for his paper. It used to be that his cousins and uncle were in here with him. Then they found their maá all the way on the other side of the world, waiting for them where it snows all day and all night. Before they left, Eli's uncle promised that Eli would join them – they just had to get through some more paperwork first, is all.

When that Jacket calls out Eli's number, Eli's face explodes into a smile. And my chest is bursting with a hurting kind of happiness, thinking of Eli dancing in the snow with his family, and I smile right back.

When Eli's cousin left, Eli told him, 'Where you're going, you won't last an hour without freezing right up, and then the only thing to save you is hot chocolate so sweet and hot it burns your throat and thaws you out from the inside.' And when they said goodbye and walked through the gates, their smiles were so big, the happiness steamed right up out of them and into the sky. It snuck up our noses and ears, and we waved goodbye and we smiled and called out and breathed in that happiness. And Eli stood behind me and kept his hands on my shoulders and whispered in my ear how, one day, the two of us would be hot-chocolate chefs and world-famous ones, so that people would come from all over just to taste what we'd made. And after they had gone so far we couldn't even make out their shadows driving away, we all of us still smiled, feeling that snow crunching between our toes, and the hot chocolate burning in our throats.

But Eli isn't going to the snow.

'Get your stuff,' the Jacket said. 'You're moving to Alpha.'

It's Queeny who talks first. 'But that's for the single men.'

The Jacket sniffs and doesn't even look like he's heard. Eli and Queeny and me, we all just look at each other, because none of it makes sense.

'I said get your stuff. You're too old to be in Family. Now move it, boy.'

This time Queeny steps so she's right in front of the Jacket. 'Eli isn't no man. He's still a good five years off going to Alpha, and you know it.'

I pull on Queeny, trying to get her to step back because it's no use the both of us getting shoved twice in two days, but the Jacket just slaps his paper on Queeny's cheek.

'That's not what his paper says. He was meant to move last week. And writing doesn't lie.'

But I can tell that even the Jacket knows that the paper is lying better than anyone.

Eli shrugs. All three of us are thinking the same thing. Thinking about the other boy, the one who was only nine, but his paper said he was nineteen. Everyone could see as clear as day that there was no way this kid was nineteen, but those Jackets still went and put him over in Alpha. 'It's there in black and white on the paper,' they said.

And something happens to those men when they live all together like that, without their families, without being able to work or learn or do anything, having to listen to the Jackets and their jangling keys all the time. It changes a person, Eli says. Some of those men can be real mean to a kid when they want to be.

I can see all that working its way through Eli's brain, just the same way it's working its way through mine, because both of us saw what happened to that boy when he'd eventually been let into Family. By then, it was too late, is all. After he tried to bleed himself out on the fence, they moved him to Ford, his brain so mushed that he wasn't even really there.

Writing does lie. It lies all the time.

Eli shrugs at me again and smiles, trying his best not to show his scared even though I can see from the shake in his hands that he isn't sure it will be OK, no matter what his shoulders shrug. 'They should really just let us kids run things, hey, Subhi?' he grins. 'More brains.'

He taps his head with his finger, right up close to the Jacket's face when he says it so there is no confusing what he means by it.

'There would at least be more ice cream,' I say. I laugh, trying to get the Jacket to think Eli is just having fun so he'll let go of his fistful of Eli's shirt and walk away with no more bother. 'And lamb.' Now the Jacket is looking at me, so I keep talking, talking, talking. 'I've only ever had lamb once and even though I felt kind of bad eating an animal that was only still a baby itself, it tasted just perfect. Do you remember, Eli? Do you remember, Queeny? When we had lamb? Do you remember?' I'm asking the Jacket even though I know for sure he wasn't here that time we had lamb.

The Jacket shakes his head and lets go of Eli, cuffing him hard across the ear so that Eli loses his balance and ends up on the dirt.

'You've got five minutes to get your crap together. There better not be any trouble.' The Jacket looks at all three of us now, his finger pointing. Eli just grins right up at that Jacket like he's telling the best joke Eli's ever heard. 'Because if there is so much as a pip out of you, BER-18, I'll be moving you to Beta instead. You got that?'

Beta, where they lock you up and don't let you out. Beta, where you don't have anyone to look out for you at all. I tell the Jacket yes sir we've got that sir and we'll be no trouble at all mister sir. Eli stands up and smiles his big smile at the Jacket and when the Jacket turns around to go, Eli blows him a kiss.

I wish Eli wouldn't do stuff like that. It makes me want to vomit every time. But the Jacket doesn't hear, and if he does he keeps walking and my heart goes back to beating quietly instead of thundering in my ears. I turn to Eli. 'If us kids ran the world, there would be ice cream every day and roast lamb with mint sauce and potatoes once a month, and so much water that we could all drink until our stomachs were just about to burst.'

'And grilled fish with vegetables pulled straight from the ground,' Queeny adds.

'And hot-chocolate rain falling from the sky.' Eli looks up to the sky to check it hasn't already started to fall. He sticks his tongue out of his mouth and closes his eyes. 'I reckon I can taste it already . . .' he says. Then he breathes in all the smells from the camp, long and deep through his nose – the rubbish rotting in the line of bins just the other side of the fence, the pipe from the toilet leaking into the dirt, some vomit where someone couldn't handle whatever breakfast was – and Eli's imagining crumples into the dirt.

'The rain needs some work,' he says, and we all laugh. When Eli says that they'll see their mistake soon enough, we start laughing again and Eli chokes on his own spit, but none of us really thinks it's that funny.

Just when that Jacket is coming back into the tent to

take Eli, I reach into my pocket and give him one of the oldest of my treasures. It's the rock, all the way from space. Harvey taught me all about space and rocks. He said that the black and the bubbles in the rock show that it's from a shooting star, come all the way down to earth. I give it to Eli so he can make a wish on it. I don't tell him that I already tried a wish but it didn't work because my ba is still out there and we are still in here. I figure that maybe shooting-star wishes only work for certain people, and Eli, he's the kind of person a shooting-star wish would work for.

It's not until that night that I realise I never got to tell Eli about the girl. I try to draw a picture of the girl on the other side of the paper from The Night Sea With Creatures, but the girl looks all whispery and not quite there on the page. I try to stop thinking about Eli not being in Family with me because that blots the picture and makes it worse. Someday we'll be together again. Just not today, is all.

Even though I can't draw her right, I can see the girl in my head. There is something in her that makes me feel like I've met her before. As I'm falling asleep, I wonder if maybe my ba has sent the girl. If he has, I wish he would stop being so damn confusing and just send his own goddamn self. It can't be that bloody hard.

I keep on thinking of the girl and my ba sending me his treasures until my brain stops and drifts me to sleep. I keep thinking on it so I don't have to think about Eli.

9

Jimmie rolls the name around her tongue. 'Subhi.' She likes it. He was kind of quiet, but he seemed nice. And she liked that he talked to a rubber duck. Jimmie's mum used to talk to her garden gnome whenever she went outside. She said they were some of the most interesting conversations she had.

Jimmie picks up the leather notebook. 'Subhi can read,' she says to its cover. There's just the slightest touch of a smile in Jimmie's voice.

When Jimmie hears the front door open and Jonah's voice singing along to the music blaring in his ears, she feels an excitement and a happiness buzz through her.

'You're not wasting my bike money on your stupid music, are you?' Jimmie grabs Jonah's hands and swings him around.

Jonah grunts and pushes Jimmie to the ground, chuckling as he does it.

'It's not long until my birthday, and bikes are expensive,' she says.

'What bike? I don't have any money for a bike, Turd Head.'

For a moment, Jimmie's brain freezes. For a moment, that buzzing goes so quiet that there is just hard silence pumping in her ears. She can feel a wave of heat starting in her cheeks.

But then Jonah starts laughing so hard that the chocolate milk he's drinking dribbles out of his open mouth and on to the floor. 'You should have seen your face!' he howls.

Jimmie thinks about grabbing the milk and pouring it on his head. That's the kind of thing that used to drive her parents nuts. They'd look at whatever disaster she'd caused and say, 'Jimmie! You have to stop and think! What did you expect would happen?'

Jimmie's mum used to call her Cyclone Jimmie. 'You're so loud and . . . and . . . chaotic! You just charge along and suck up space as you go.' She always said it with a smile, though, and a curious look like she couldn't quite work Jimmie out and was glad for it.

But Jimmie was older now, and anyway, they didn't have much milk left. She'd get Jonah back later. 'I knew you were joking,' Jimmie says. Jonah snorts so hard that chocolate milk comes out his nose.

Jimmie makes herself a chocolate milk then, and when Jonah isn't looking, she spits in his milk and stirs it in. She'll tell him later, after he's drunk it all down. He'll think it was funny.

When Jimmie goes back to her room, she flicks through the pages of the book again, her fingers feeling the raised ink where her mum had written down all those words. A bike would get her to the fence faster. Get her to Subhi faster. Subhi, who can read and who talks to a duck.

This time, when that buzzing excitement starts up again in her legs, it doesn't go away.

10

There's a group of three boys in Family Tent One. They're big. Almost grown to men. Mostly the rest of us all just keep well away from those boys. But there's just so much keeping away you can do when you're all locked in Family together.

The way Queeny tells it is that they've been here too long, is all. She reckons they used to be just like me, except maybe not so annoying.

Harvey thinks they're bored, is all. But I get bored and I don't get mean the way these boys do. I won't either, no matter how long I'm here.

Eli reckons they just aren't worth spit.

The Jackets should have taken those boys to Alpha instead of Eli.

Eli is the only one who can keep those boys from working up to crazy. He's the only one who can talk them into quiet. And it isn't just because he can get them stuff without even having to swap. Those boys would listen to Eli anyway. Eli's like that. He knows how to make people see things right.

Before Eli came to Family, when I was still little, those boys used to trap the rats. There are lots of rats here, but they mostly don't do any harm. Sometimes at night they might try a little nibble on any fingers and toes hanging out of the bed, but they run real quick when you move. Queeny, she says she woke up one night and a rat was nibbling away at her nose. I reckon she made that up to scare me.

I told Queeny to make those boys stop their trapping, but she just told me to tell them myself and stop being such a piss-pants. She said if a rat was dumb enough to fall for the trap then it deserved to die. Her face was all twisted when she said it, though.

I told Harvey about the traps but he said that anything that got rid of the rats was a good thing, and didn't I know they carried germs and disease? I told Harvey that rats were fine, and all you had to do was ask those rats not to nibble on you and give them some rice to nibble on instead. Harvey looked at me with his eyes open wide and said that he was going to pretend he didn't hear that and I wasn't going to do it any more, right? I said right, but that ruined the deal I had going with the rats, so then my fingers were in as much danger as everyone else's.

Eli, he wouldn't let those boys make their traps, though. He couldn't care about the rats, but he saw my face when I heard them squeal, and then he went and told those boys that they weren't to trap the rats any more, like there wasn't any way around it. He went and broke every one of their traps right there in front of them too.

Later, those boys hid behind the tents until Eli went for a piss and then jumped him with sticks. They didn't make the traps again, though. They even said sorry to Eli, but Eli reckons that was only because they wanted to join the package delivery business.

Mostly we all just keep away from those boys. But sometimes you can't.

I'm waiting by the fence for Eli because he didn't come like he was meant to after breakfast yesterday, and he didn't come the day before that either, and even though Harvey told me that Eli is doing just fine in Alpha, I won't believe it until I've seen him myself.

Then I see him coming, and my smile pulls at my mouth because Harvey was right. Harvey's always right. Eli is doing just fine. I can tell by his walk, all full of strong, that he's got those men worked out just like he gets everyone worked out.

'Hey, little man. Where's your shoes?'

When I don't answer, Eli puts his hand through the fence and lifts my chin so I'm looking him in the eye. Seeing him looking at me like that, I can't stop my eyes from watering and I wish more than anything that Eli was still in Family with me. Because Eli, he made everything OK.

'I couldn't stop them, Eli. I tried.' My voice is all croaking and quiet. 'They were just too big. They even took my pants.' I show him the rubber band bunching the sides together so the too-big ones Queeny scrounged for me can't fall down.

'And –' I pull my face away so I'm not looking at Eli, but down at the ants scuttling around in the dirt, not a bit bothered by us '– and they took the business too. They made me show them where the stash was. Everything.'

But Eli smiles and tells me to shush. That it doesn't matter and that he was tired of running the package delivery business anyway. 'Let 'em have it. It wouldn't have worked with me in here anyway, little bruda. I was about to come and tell you to hand it over, anyhow. And who needs shoes, hey?'

It doesn't matter that Eli is lying through his teeth, as Harvey says, because Eli, he makes everything all right.

'I guess we'll just have to make do with stealing our own underwear and water and soap when we need it,' he says, like it's the easiest thing in the world. I've already decided I'm not going to bother stealing toothpaste. It doesn't matter what Eli says. I don't reckon good teeth are worth it.

The two of us sit down in the dirt and Eli points up at the sky, right at that sun. He doesn't even blink to get the bright away. 'Sometimes, Subhi, the sun is so burning hot that it sends these massive balls of fire straight at the earth. And the fire is so strong and hot that it could destroy the whole planet. But down here on earth, we're protected, right? So all we see are beautiful lights that dance across the sky. People come from all over just to see those lights dance. You can't see them from here, not ever, but someday, Subhi, you and me, we'll go see those lights boogie through the dark, yeah?' Eli wiggles his bum in the dirt and grins. 'Hey, cheer up, bud. It could be worse. They could've put me over in Echo and then we'd be talking to each other through the toilets instead of through the fence.' He waits for me to smile, but it's not so funny. 'I'll see you tomorrow, yeah?'

Even though I wish he would stay longer, I nod.

I don't tell Eli that those boys are already making their rat traps again. I don't tell Eli that after those boys took my shoes and my pants and our packages, they walked me to a trap. I don't tell Eli how those boys pushed me right up close and showed me a little baby rat, its eyes not even open yet, sniffing around for its maá. I don't tell Eli how those boys said I was to kill it.

I told those boys to jam it. I told those boys that they could beat me with sticks as much as they wanted and I still wouldn't kill a thing. I told those boys that they weren't worth spit and then I went and broke all their traps so they'll never build them again.

Except I didn't. Except I couldn't. I don't tell Eli. And after, when I wiped that blood and fur off my hands and on to the dirt, the rats, all hidden in the shadows, watched me and shook their heads and turned away.

I don't tell Eli any of that. Instead I say, 'See ya tomorrow, then,' and watch him strong walk back to his tent.

I spend the next five nights watching the sky, watching for those lights to dance. Even though Eli says we can't see them from here, not ever, Maá always used to tell me that sometimes 'not ever' can change.

It doesn't, though. Not for me.

It's been eight nights now. Eight nights since the girl came. Eight nights of lying in my bed pretending to sleep, my breath sucking in with waiting until the breathing in the rest of the tent slows and most of the eyes have shut enough to not care if I'm in my bed or not. Eight nights of sitting outside with no Night Sea and no dancing lights and no girl, just red dirt going on and on for ever and ever.

'And me,' the duck says. 'Don't forget eight nights of my sparkling wit and fascinating conversation.'

But I know that duck is as twitchy as me, waiting to see if the girl is as real as we remember her. Harvey says sometimes your brain can play tricks on your eyes – and ears too, I guess – and ever since that night I've been trying to work out if that girl is a trick or real.

I still haven't told Eli about her. We don't get much time alone to talk now that he's in Alpha. He's made sure to meet me at the fence every day, and we chat, but it's not like before. Now, wherever we are, there are eyes on us and ears pricked, even though nothing we've got to say is very interesting anyway.

Maybe I am going crazy. Maybe a cockroach has climbed all the way in my ears like they do sometimes, except this time I didn't notice quick enough to get the doc to tweezer it out. Maybe it climbed all the way in and all the way down to my brain and it's making me see and hear things.

Just as I'm telling the duck that I've had about enough of waiting and I must be going crazy thinking some girl could have magicked right through those fences when there's no way she could have done, and the Shakespeare duck is saying right back that the only crazy bit is sitting and talking to a rubber duck, then there she is. As real and beautiful as I remember, even in the deep dark.

'That's her!' the Shakespeare duck quacks. I reckon he's more excited even than me. 'Don't forget to find out her name this time,' he reminds me. He's getting kind of bossy for a rubber duck.

The girl sits down next to me and wipes her nose on her arm so the silver trail from it glints in the light from the moon. 'Is that your duck?' she asks, her voice all whispery so we won't be heard.

When I don't answer, she nods like I've explained the whole lot myself. She twirls a big black feather around and around in her fingers and all I can do is watch the way that feather spins through the dark, like it has its own light shining up out of it.

'So, how long have you been in here for?'

'For ever,' I say, my shoulders shrugging off her question like it makes no difference. 'I was born here.'

After that she doesn't say much for a bit, just keeps twirling that feather around while I watch. It catches the light from the moon, a smudge of a whole rainbow of colours caught inside that one feather.

'What about your family?'

'I've got a sister, Queeny, but she's pretty rubbish mostly. And my maá. And my dad is on his way, but not here yet. And Eli is my best friend and just as good as a brother. Better than Queeny.'

The girl nods some more. 'My mum's dead,' she says. 'She got this fever one time and something in her brain just popped, that's how the doctors said. And that was it. She was just dead, sitting right there on the bathroom floor.'

'Oh,' I say, and try not to think what that might have looked like.

'I also have a brother, Jonah. He's sixteen and meant to be in charge when my dad works his long shifts. Jonah's not much good at it, though. When his friends come around they always end up drinking too much beer and he forgets that he's meant to look out for me. He's an all-right brother, though. He always brings me a chocolate bar to say sorry, and he's going to get me a bike for my birthday. He promised. And anyway, I wouldn't really care about being on my own, except that there's no one else around for miles. Sometimes I think that there's someone outside coming to get me, and that no one would hear my screams. I guess maybe I've watched too many horror movies with Jonah. Oh. I'm Jimmie, by the way.' She picks up my hand and shakes it up and down. 'Nice to meet ya.'

From inside my pocket I hear the duck say, 'My, my. She's quite the talker, isn't she?'

'Anyway.' Jimmie pulls out a torch from her pocket. It's much smaller than the ones the Jackets carry, but when she turns it on, it flashes a light so bright that I grab at it and shove it down into the dirt.

'Someone'll see!' I hiss. 'Only the Jackets have torches.' It's a good thing that Jimmie can't hear the duck talking, because what he's saying isn't particularly friendly.

'Well, where can we go then?'

The two of us look at each other and I get to feeling that maybe I'm not understanding this girl so well, because I have no idea what she's talking about.

'Go?' I say.

Then she reaches into her pocket and waves her book under my face.

I've read everything there is to read in Family, even the books with the endings ripped out and the magazines from before I was born and the stuff I don't really understand and the stuff that's really boring, like the folder with emergency phone numbers and instructions. Once I got so bursting to read that I swiped the instruction manual for fitting out the new container block for the Rec Room. By the time I finished, I was even more bored than when I started. But I could see straight off where the Outside men had built it all wrong. They always use Outside men to build stuff even though people in here want to help. We're not allowed to use tools.

'To read my mum's stories. You said you could read.' Jimmie looks at me now, as though maybe I can't read, as though maybe I tricked her. 'I don't have long, 'K?' She stands and pulls me up by my shirt. At least she's turned her torch off.

The only place I can think to go is to the blind spot over by Alpha. I haven't been back to that corner since Beaver found me, but at least the cameras can't see and the bushes will hide the torchlight.

'Come on then,' I say. I take Jimmie's wrist in the dark and lead her around the back of the tents, keeping right close to the canvas so we can't be spotted in the shadows. The duck shouts at me from my pocket: 'Are you sure this is sensible? This doesn't seem very sensible. It's only a book of stories. I can tell you a story when you're nice and safe and tucked up in bed. Listen, here we go. *Once upon a time there was a duck . . .*'

But knowing that Jimmie has a whole real book in her hands gives me a sort of brave that I haven't felt since Eli got taken. My fingers are tingling just thinking about touching those pages.

I pull Jimmie into the corner and lean against the brick, still warm from being soaked in the sun all day. Now that I've stopped, my legs start shaking and I have to squeeze them together to keep them still. I guess they aren't feeling as brave as the rest of me. From here we can see the Jackets' Rec Room and can spot their torches as soon as they come out for their rounds. I'll have time to scoot around back to Family Tent Three and get into bed before they've even left Family One. I reckon Jimmie will be OK on her own – she seems like the kind of kid to have a plan.

We sit down in the dirt, squashed in together behind the bush, and Jimmie stares at the book in her hands for a while. 'It's Mum's.'

She's said that already, but I don't say. I wonder how it would feel to have a book of my ba's stories and poems and no ba to tell them, not ever. Not even Someday.

Jimmie keeps staring at the book like she's trying to decide if she's ready to hand it over or not. The cover of the book is torn and the pages are all brown and curling over from its being so old and touched. The whole thing is stitched together with string that seems thin enough to break just from being looked at.

'This was Mum's too.'

The girl fiddles with something hanging around her neck. I shine the torch on it, just for a second, my fingers covering most of the light. It's a bird, its wings spread out and flying high on the wind. The only thing I can think of is the bird sitting waiting for me on my pillow and what Queeny said that meant. When Jimmie says, 'It's a sparrow carved from bone,' my breath pulls in tight. I drop the torch and move away so quickly that my head smacks back on the brick wall Beaver shoved me into and sends a sick feeling all the way down to my toes.

Jimmie looks at the scared on my face and laughs. 'It's not that bad. Although I guess his eye is kind of creepy.'

She picks up the torch and shines it back on the bird, and even though I don't want to look, my eyes are sucking it up and holding me there. That bone bird makes me feel strange all over, and my brain gets to thinking that Queeny is right, that the sparrow in the house meant death and here it is, come to collect me now. I can feel my skin turning cold and wet. A tingle creeps up my neck and makes me shiver, even with my back right up against the hot of those bricks, and I wonder if maybe I shouldn't be sitting out here in the dark by myself with a girl I don't know, wearing a symbol of death around her neck.

The duck hisses, 'I told you so! But you never listen. No, no, no,' and now I can feel my throat catching, so that when I try to talk my voice comes out all wobbly and strangled.

'Does it mean death or something?'

Jimmie just laughs.

'Course not. Why would it? Because it's bone? Mum said it gives us luck and protection. She said all the souls of everyone in our family, all our stories and everything, rub right into that bone and he keeps us together. But then she went and died. That's pretty crappy protection in my opinion and not very good luck. It's probably just a stupid story anyway.'

'So why do you wear it?' I ask.

'I guess, just in case, maybe? Maybe if Mum wasn't wearing it, she would have died even sooner. Maybe it's a different kind of luck. I don't know, do I?'

I have nothing to say to that. For a moment, we're just quiet. Neither one saying a thing, and that quiet ballooning up and filling the air around us. My breath has gone back to normal, and my heart isn't pounding quite so hard, but I'm still not sure about that bird.

Finally, I touch the book. 'Jimmie? Can we read some of your mum's stories now?'

And without saying another word, Jimmie hands me the book and closes her eyes to listen.

II

This is a tale from long, long ago.
Anka was born from an egg.

I stop reading and look at Jimmie. This is just the kind of story that would drive Queeny wild. She'd scream and rage about how stupid it was, and that no one could be born from an egg, and why would you waste head space with stuff like that? But Jimmie is staring at me with a kind of hungry in her eyes, one fist clenched tight around the Bone Sparrow and her other hand still twirling her feather. Jimmie isn't anything like Queeny.

'Anka was my great-great-great-grandmother,' she says. 'Hurry up, will you? Stories don't work if you stop all the time. Don't you know about reading?'

Maybe she is like Queeny, just a bit.

No one knew where she had come from. But there she was, cradled by a nest, half way down the old well, with fragments of broken shell sticking to her hair and skin. Some people thought she had been dropped by a passing traveller, happy to be rid of a child covered in hair that looked more like feathers than the soft hair of a newborn babe.

'Leave it down there,' spat Guntis. He was the oldest man in the town, although certainly not the wisest. But in a town where age was respected above wisdom, his word was often

obeyed. His nose was red and blistered from too many summers under the hot sun, and he walked with a stick used often to prod others into action. 'Who are we to mess with the gods? Pah.' He shook his head as he peered down at the mewling child stuck in the well, and scowled.

'What nonsense you talk, Old Man,' said Mirka. 'This is clearly the work of a person, not a god. Now stop your talking and someone get that child out of there so we can all go home.'

Guntis may have been the oldest man in the town, but Mirka was the oldest woman. Her nose wasn't quite as red as Guntis', despite having spent more summers in the sun than her brother. And she was certainly considered wise. She was also the only one who could override her brother's decision.

The townspeople jumped into action. The only one small and thin enough to fit down the well was Oto, a six-year-old boy. Slowly, Oto was lowered by rope into the well, where he picked up the baby and held her tightly to his chest. An undeniable surge of love for the girl filled Oto's chest. Before he had even been pulled back from the darkness of the well, he had vowed to protect this child, no matter what she might face.

As Oto and the baby came into the light,

Oto raised his chin in determination. 'Her name is Anka,' he said, and his eyes flashed, daring anyone to argue.

Guntis and Mirka looked at each other. There was no question in either of their minds as to the fate of the two children, destined to follow a path strewn with hardships. Guntis looked down at Anka, cradled in the arms of the small boy. 'Pft.' He spat a wet glob of chewed tobacco on to the ground by Oto's feet. 'She's as blind as a bat, that one. She'll never see a thing.' And he shook his head again and walked away.

It was only Mirka, who knew her brother too well, who saw him cast a final look back at the children, with a mixture of hope and sadness etched across his face.

Mirka picked a piece of shell from the baby's hair. 'He's right,' she said. 'The girl is blind. But, Oto,' she lowered her voice so that only the boy could hear, 'this girl is destined to see more than most.' And with that, she followed her brother out of the town square.

I turn the page but the story stops. How can someone do that? Stop a story just like that? The next page is a list written in blue pen of the top ten places to visit before you die. I wonder how many Jimmie's mum had visited.

Jimmie looks at the Bone Sparrow in her hands. Her cheeks are glinting wet.

'Should I keep reading?' I ask, fingering the pages to try and find more of the story while all the words wash through my head. I can see the baby down the well, and the feathers all over it, and the little boy Oto cradling that babe in his arms.

But Jimmie shakes her head. 'I want to save the stories. Make them last long, you know?'

I nod, and she stands up and says, 'All right then.' She takes back the book and the torch from me and hands me her feather instead. 'Thanks, Subhi.'

And then she leaves, disappearing into the dark and the dirt, and the moon disappears with her.

Watching her go, something in my chest explodes. Now there's a tightness in there that I can't shake, no matter how many breaths I suck in, and an exciting rush in my legs, tingling through to my toes.

I wonder when Jimmie'll come back.

From my pocket, I hear the Shakespeare duck. 'And the duck was the most magnificent duck the world had ever seen . . .'

12

Jimmie stops outside the fence and lets the story work its way through her mind. Jimmie's mum had told her that story so many times that she knew the words by heart. But this was the first time since her mum's death that she had thought to remember it. The first time that she had heard the whisper of her mum's voice. It was perfect.

Jonah had told their mum that those stories were rubbish, and Jimmie had echoed him, trying to sound tough and grown-up like her brother. 'Ah, but it was back in the old country,' her mum had said. 'And a long time ago. Don't forget, things were different back then. Back then, anything was possible.'

Jonah had only laughed and Jimmie had joined in, and after a while her mum stopped trying to tell them the stories. Jimmie hated that she'd done that to her mum. But her mum must have known somehow that Jimmie did believe. Because the nights when Jimmie helicoptered on her bed, trying to find sleep, her mum had come and whispered the stories to her, her fingers tracing patterns on her back until her body settled and she fell asleep.

Jimmie lets the bone touch her lips and squeezes the book against her chest before heading back up the hill.

That night, tucked safely in bed, Jimmie can't stop smiling. And for the first time in three years, Jimmie sleeps the long, deep sleep of someone who has finally found what they are looking for.

13

It's still dark when Harvey comes in. 'Happy birthday, kiddo.' He says it so soft, I know he doesn't want me to wake up, but I'm already awake, thinking of Jimmie and her book of stories.

I wait until Harvey's gone, feeling the weight of something on my legs. Even though it's too dark to see, I know what the present from Harvey is. I know because every year since turning five, he brings me the same perfect gift, sneaking it in to the tent so no one knows who left it.

My fingers pull at the box and slide over the top of the pencils. Twelve colours, itching at me to start drawing, and a whole book full of empty white, waiting to be filled. Harvey told me once that when he was a kid he thought he was going to be an artist like his dad. He doesn't tell me how he ended up here instead.

And without seeing, because of the dark, I draw.

When the light is strong enough to wake us up, I open my eyes and look at my picture. That feather, it has all the colours pushing out of the page right at me. Even the colours that pencils aren't made in.

Queeny wakes up and sings me Happy Birthday. She reaches under her pillow and pulls out a pair of pants.

'These ones will fit better. They're from Maá.'

Maá is still asleep, rolled over on her side so she doesn't wake. And when I kiss her cheek, just the whisper of a word comes out. I'm pretty sure she is saying Happy Birthday in Rohingya.

Maá doesn't come to breakfast, though. I guess she still isn't hungry much.

There must be a bit of birthday luck flying about the place, because when Queeny and I get our breakfast, we know straight away what it is. There's no playing Guess the Food this morning, because our plates are piled high with scrambled eggs and toast. Real eggs and real toast. We both look at each other and smile. We've got Guests in the camp today.

'Government people,' Queeny says, her mouth open and the egg flying in spits on to the table. But I reckon it's the Human Rightsers. The food is always the tastiest when they come, and this is just about the best I can remember. I wish Maá was here to taste it. I look down at my food so Queeny doesn't see my eyes filling.

I don't even wait for Queeny to finish. As soon as I've had my last mouthful, I'm out of the tent and running towards the fence. I need to tell Eli about Jimmie and the stories. He said he'd be here waiting for me after breakfast to say happy birthday. But when I get to the fence the only thing there is a small piece of string, tied in a bow. I tie it around my finger and wait, until the sun gets that hot that I can't see right. I guess Eli got held up. Or distracted, is all. I guess I'll tell him later.

But that bored is getting to me now. Grinding at me. I sit outside for a while and watch the drops of sweat race down my elbow. I keep picking the losing sweat drop, though. I hate this feeling of not knowing what to do. I never felt like this when Eli was in Family with me. Eli always had something going on. I start Fence Walking, thinking on Jimmie, and I've just finished my fourth lap when Nasir calls me over to Family Three.

Nasir lives in Family Three with us. He's one of the oldest in here. He's been here the longest of anyone too. He's here with his granddaughter and nephew now, but when he first came, he was all alone for a long time. I guess it must have smudged him up to see other people come and go and wonder why he couldn't. The Jackets say he has an 'adverse risk assessment'. But the Jackets also say they can't send him back to where he came from because he's been given refugee status. So he's stuck. Stuck in the camp until they decide he's not a risk any more. They don't even say why he's a risk, or what he's supposed to have done. Now almost none of us get sent anywhere, so I guess now we're all smudging up and wondering why together. Some days Nasir is just how he used to be, but other days he gets confused. His brain isn't so sharp any more, is the way Harvey puts it. 'A few bricks shy of a load,' he says.

When I was really little, I would curl up in Nasir's lap, and me and Maá would talk with him for hours. Maá would tell him things, all about places and people, and even though Nasir didn't know who or where Maá was talking about, he would still nod and smile and say, 'I remember.' Nasir understands that sometimes memories have to be made. He also tells the best stories of anyone in the camp and showed us kids a whole bunch of games to play when the days get too long and the same, and taught us how to build dams when it rains, to trap the water.

Nasir smiles when I come over. 'Happy birthday, my Subhi!' he says in his soft croak.

I can tell straight off from the way he's talking that he's having a good day today. His eyes smile along with his mouth, and even with that ache of sad about them, there isn't the wide-open scared that he gets when he can't remember where he is or why he's here or where the rest of his family is.

'Hey, Nasir,' I say. 'Did you get to breakfast today?'

Nasir nods. 'Human Rights Watch, I think,' he says, and licks his lips. 'I sure they be round soon 'nough to take their notes. Are you having good day?'

I shrug, thinking of Eli, my eyes watching Maá, still asleep, and Nasir leans over and squeezes my shoulder. 'Come sit with me, Subhi.'

Nasir hops on his crutch over to his bed. He's only got one leg. He used to have a plastic one to go with his real one but the Jackets took that away when he got here and never gave it back. Nasir says he doesn't mind so much about his leg. He says it is worse for people like Fara, who is deaf and had her hearing aid taken, so that now she can't hear the memories people tell each other to keep themselves alive in here. Or the ones like Remi, who needs medicine every day and had that taken away by the Jackets, and even the letter from his doctor was destroyed. Remi has these fits and headaches that make him scream so hard it cuts through your thinking. He says all he needs is his medicine. 'I thought you would help me.' He says that over and over again. I don't know who he's talking to, though.

When I sit down, Nasir shuffles around in his things. 'I have present. For you.' He hands me a small stone. Black and shiny and as smooth as silk. I know how smooth silk is because once Nasir took me with him when he went to look through his Belongings Box. He showed me his wife's scarf which was silk and all he had to remind him of her. He didn't have anything else in his Belongings Box and it seemed kind of silly to me to go to all the trouble of filling in the forms and waiting to be put on the list so we could look through his belongings if there was only one thing to look at. But that scarf was super smooth and full of colours, and even though when I smelled it, it just smelled of wet and mould and rats, when Nasir smelled it, he said it still smelled of his wife.

I know right off what the stone is. It's a Pebble of Happy. Nasir taught me all about them too.

'Thank you, Nasir. It's wonderful.'

And it really is. I do it just like Nasir taught me. I hold that pebble in my hand and think of the happiest thought I can. Each pebble can only hold one thought, so I have to think of the best one right off. I try to think of my dad and the places we'll go and the things we'll do when he gets here, but instead my brain takes over and suddenly I'm thinking of Jimmie and of a baby born from an egg, and I'm feeling that excited waiting right down in my belly, thinking when I might see her again.

This is my fifth Pebble of Happy. They're hard to find. But I think this is just about the happiest pebble I have. Nasir must know because he's smiling at me and laughing the soft laugh of his that makes me feel safe all over when I hear it.

'Now every time you hold your pebble, you remember your think and smile.'

I know I will too.

After that, Nasir and I talk a bit and I tell him all about Eli getting moved to Alpha. Nasir shakes his head and looks so sad that I wish I had never mentioned it. We must have been sat there for a while chatting, because pretty soon Nasir's eyes start to get that blurry look and I can feel him smudging up. Queeny said I should just leave him be when he's like that, but I think Nasir likes me being there with him because when I put his hand on mine he doesn't move it away.

I sit with him and tell him back some of the stories he's told me and I get the Pebbles of Happy Nasir has for himself and close his hand around them so he can feel his own happy thoughts. When I've done that, he stops whimpering and falls asleep, his pebbles in one hand, and his other holding my fingers so tight that it hurts. I lean in close then, and I tell him all about Jimmie, and all about her book. 'I'll tell you every story there is in that book, Nasir. I promise.'

Just before I leave, I put Jimmie's feather in his hand so he'll see the colours when he wakes up. I bet he knows a bunch of games with feathers.

And that night, I lean into Maá and tell her all about my birthday. 'They made me scrambled eggs for breakfast, Maá, and we had real fruit at lunch and sausages for dinner. I saved my second sausage for you, Maá. It's here if you get hungry. Harvey says they did that all for me, Maá. For my birthday.' Maá's breathing isn't heavy, and her eyes open for a bit and look at me, but I don't think she's really awake.

But then her eyes get sharper and she's looking at me, really looking at me. Her fingers come up and touch my cheek, so soft it's almost not even there, and she smiles. 'My Subhi,' she whispers. I help her to sit up and she drinks a whole half bottle of water. When I wave the sausage under her nose, though, she pushes it away with her hand. 'I'll put it under your pillow so the rats don't get it, OK, Maá?' She doesn't say OK, but she doesn't stop me either.

Then she looks at me and says, 'Is it rain?'

And it is. Rain. Real rain. The kind that pours from the sky like it will never end. The kind that thumps through your body and pounds on your head with those big fat drops that splat and tickle down your face and into your ears.

I link Maá's arm through mine and help her out into the rain and we stand there, the two of us, not even noticing all the others about, laughing and calling up to the sky. We stand there, letting that rain soak into us.

'Long time back,' Maá says, her voice quiet, 'there no rain here, in this country. Many years, no rain. Then you be born, Subhi, and that rain fall from sky. Just like this. Just like it be waiting to flood on you head. Just like whole country waiting. Just for you.' Maá looks at me again, her smile big and wide this time, so I can see it for sure, even through the tired. I've never heard that story before.

Then the bell rings for curfew and the Jackets come around to check our ID numbers, and Maá goes back to bed. She says she needs some sleep. Before she lies down, I check under her pillow, but the sausage is already gone.

Maá lies down, and her eyes close and she sighs.

'Maá?' I whisper. 'I measured. I'm twenty-one fence diamonds high. Maá?'

But now her breathing is slow and she's definitely asleep again.

'Maá? Can you tell me one of your Listen Now stories? Just the one?'

She doesn't answer. I didn't think she would.

14

We're waiting for Jimmie, me and the Shakespeare duck. We sit back in the blind-spot corner while we wait. Even though we didn't say it last time, I figure this will be where she comes. I hope so anyway, because I've been waiting here the last three nights with the duck. And now my brain is starting to peck at me that maybe she won't come back.

While we're waiting, I'm showing the duck how to play Towers of Rah. I'm up to eleven stones, which is my record so far. Eli is the champion. He got twenty-three stones balanced once. The duck says it's not much of a game, but he doesn't have any hands to balance rocks with, so I don't think he really gets it.

There's a trick to the balancing. You've got to find the right stones. The long, flat ones balance best but are hardest to find. A big, heavy one on the bottom of the stack helps too. Big stones are also good if you're going for the highest tower instead of the most stones, but little ones are good if you can balance them on the side of a bigger stone because then they count for more.

My favourite game with stones is Target. That's where a big stone is thrown and then you have to try and get your little stones as close as you can to the big one. I'm best at that. Even better than Eli, although Queeny said he was just letting me win, which I reckoned was probably right because Eli didn't ever get beaten by anyone else. I asked Queeny if she was just letting me win as well and she didn't answer. That means no.

I've just balanced fourteen rocks and even the duck is getting a bit excited, saying, 'Go, kid! You are on a roll!' when Jimmie appears and makes me jump so that I knock over my tower before I can balance number fifteen.

'Whoops. Sorry!' she whispers.

Even though I've been trying all my life to get to fifteen because Queeny's record is fourteen, I couldn't give a damn about that tower when I see Jimmie.

It's not just the book and torch she's brought tonight, but a Thermos as well. I know about Thermoses, because some days the Jackets bring them in filled with wonderful smells that I never knew even existed, and they sip away at those smells and yo-yo their keys, and all I can do is watch. Queeny gets right mad when they do that, but that just makes them laugh. They don't laugh with their eyes, though, and soon enough they move away or put the lids back on the Thermoses. I don't mind it. With smells, if you close your eyes and breathe as deep as you can, they turn into a taste right at the back of your throat, and then you can almost pretend that the Thermos was brought in for you as well.

'Hiya,' Jimmie says, and her whole face shines like someone's lit a candle in her cheeks. 'I brought some hot chocolate.' As she takes off the lid, the steam whispers away into the night. I wonder if it's as good as the hot chocolate Eli told me about. I wonder if that steam will make it all the way into the clouds. If it did, then it really would rain down hot chocolate, like Eli said.

'I've got a joke for the duck,' Jimmie says. 'What do you call a box of ducks?'

The duck doesn't answer. He's just sat there pretending he's an everyday ordinary rubber duck. 'What?' I ask instead and Jimmie turns back to me. 'A box of quackers.'

I don't get it, even when she explains to me why it's funny.

'All right then. Another. What do you call a duck who steals?'

Even though I didn't get the last joke, my mouth is already smiling in waiting. 'What?'

'A robber duck.' Now I'm laughing for real.

'What grows down as it grows up?' I ask her back.

It only takes Jimmie a second before she answers. 'Duh. A duck. Kind of obvious.'

I don't tell her it took me a whole week and a bunch of clues from Harvey before I worked that one out.

Jimmie passes me the Thermos and I let the hot chocolate bump against my lips and dribble on to my tongue. The sweet is so strong it fills my mouth with a cloud of warm that sets my tongue tingling. It's nothing like I've ever tasted, and I close my eyes and tell my brain to remember this for ever. Then, without meaning to, my mouth is gulping at the hot chocolate, not pausing for even a breath until I see that Jimmie is laughing at me and I have hot chocolate running down the corners of my mouth and dripping into the dirt. 'Good thing I brought the big Thermos,' she says, and takes it from me. 'Watch this, then.'

Jimmie takes a sip from the Thermos, closes her eyes and moves her jaw in and out, and then hot chocolate streams out of her nose. She smiles and lets it dribble back into her mouth before she chokes from laughing.

She says she could teach me, but there isn't a snowflake's chance in hell, as Harvey says, that I'm about to waste my hot chocolate by making it come out of my nose. I tell her to pull my finger instead, which was something Eli did to me once, but Jimmie already knows that one. I thought Eli had made it up.

Then Jimmie brings out a black pen. 'Do you want a tattoo?' she says. I nod, even though I don't really want one. 'You can't look until it's finished, OK?'

She pulls the sleeve of my shirt all the way up. The pen scratches at the skin on my arm, and I bite my lip to stop from telling her that it hurts. She takes her time. When she's done, I look down at what she's drawn.

'It's meant to be a dragon but it kind of looks more like a duck. Sorry about that.'

The duck cheers from my pocket.

'I think it looks like a dragon,' I say, and looking at it upside down it really does. Kind of.

'It's meant to be like this dragon poster I have in my room,' Jimmie says, looking at the tattoo with her eyebrows bunched. 'Maybe I should have practised first . . .'

In my head I'm trying to imagine a room with a dragon poster, but all I can imagine is a container room like the ones in Hard Road. 'What's it like?' I say. 'Your room?'

Jimmie looks at me then, her face sort of squished. When she answers, her voice is all soft, like she's not sure she really wants to be telling. 'Well, I have my bed in the corner, and when I'm lying on the bed I can look out the window to our back garden and the washing line. I have four pillows on my bed and a photo of my mum on the drawers next to it. I have the dragon poster and my other stuff, like my footy and my school bag.' She shrugs. 'That's kind of it. And the walls are green.'

But I want more. When other people tell me their stories, they're from far away. Stories from other countries and other times. Stories of getting here. But no one has a story from just Outside. None of us knows what it is like just the other side of the fences. But Jimmie does.

'What about Outside? Past the fences? What's there?'

And this time when Jimmie tells me, her voice isn't soft any more. This time there is an excitement in her voice and a light in her eyes. 'I'll show you all over someday, Subhi,' Jimmie says. 'I know this place better than anyone. And someday I'll take you everywhere there is to take and we'll explore together everything there is to explore. I promise, OK?'

When I nod, Jimmie nods back. I know for sure that Jimmie is the kind of person that keeps a promise.

Jimmie gives me the pen then and says I'm to do a tattoo on her, and to make it good because it's permanent marker. The duck says she should have mentioned that before she drew her dragon-duck all over my arm.

I draw a picture of my shell from the Night Sea and Eli's whale coming up out of it. She looks at it for a long time when I'm done, without saying anything, and I'm beginning to worry about that permanent marker bit when she says, 'I love it. I'm going to take a photo and get it done as a real tattoo when I'm older.' I don't know if she's joking or not. 'What's it from?' she asks. So I tell her Eli's story.

'A long way back, when the world was nothing but sea, there lived a whale,' I start. 'The biggest, hugest whale in the ocean. The whale was as old as the universe and as big as this whole country. Every night, the whale would rise to the surface and sing his song to the moon. One night . . .'

And I tell it just the way Eli did.

Jimmie looks at me after, and touches her tattoo. 'It's perfect,' she says.

The wind picks up and bangs away at the tents so that our voices can hardly be heard over the top of the racket it's making. Jimmie hands me the book. 'Now it's time for Mum's story,' she says.

And I read.

Oto and Anka were inseparable. From the moment the sun rose in the morning to the oranged tinge of evening, Oto and Anka were together. At first, Oto helped to raise the babe, much in the way an older cousin or brother would care for his sibling. But as time went on and Anka grew, their relationship changed. Soon Oto found that Anka was teaching him the ways of the world, rather than the other way around.

Everyone agreed that Anka was a remarkable child. 'Pah,' Guntis spat. 'She's nothing but trouble.' But even he could not stop a smile breaking out when he thought no one could see.

Mirka, too, spent many hours with the child. Anka would sit on Mirka's knee, her fingers rubbing the Bone Sparrow necklace worn around Mirka's neck as though she were committing the shape deep into the darkness of her mind.

Anka taught herself how to navigate through her sightless world by clicking her tongue against the roof of her mouth and listening for the echo to guide her. She had no fear and could easily do everything a fully sighted child could do, and more.

She had a voice that caused the goats to pause in their chewing so that they might hear her song better, a voice which folk claimed could change one's very soul. When she cooked, her food could fill even the most cold and weary traveller with a warmth and happiness that was impossible to deny.

But most astonishing was her way with people. Anka had a gift for making those around her feel entirely at peace. Without realising it, the townsfolk found themselves going out of their way for a chance encounter with the girl. Although the town had previously been small, with Anka's arrival, it was as if the town sprang up around her. By the time she was eight years old, the township had more than tripled in size. It was a happy place.

As Oto and Anka grew, so did their love for each other. So it was no surprise to anyone when they announced at the beginning of Anka's sixteenth year that they were to be married.

Oto felt that they had truly lived a charmed life. They had only been married a few years when Anka's belly began to swell with the promise of new life, and Oto felt a sense of happiness and peace flood every part of his being.

So, when Mirka arrived one night to tell the pair that the time had come to leave the town they had lived in all their lives and to seek their future elsewhere, Anka and Oto merely smiled and shook their heads.

'I am too old to travel, but you are the future. Sometimes you need to walk your journey to find peace,' Mirka pleaded. Even as she did so, she knew the ears of the young ones were deaf to her knowledge.

'We already have everything we could wish for right here,' Oto said. 'Perhaps in a few years, when the babe is old enough to travel, then we could venture out, couldn't we, Anka?'

Anka smiled her radiant smile, her hand resting on her stomach. 'Of course. It's just that now isn't the right time.'

Both Oto and Anka were fond of Mirka, but she was old now, and they wondered if her perception of the world was deteriorating. They were both well aware of the war which was slowly eating its way across the country, but their town was so small and remote it seemed implausible that anyone would venture this far.

Mirka nodded. She had tried.

Later, Oto and Anka would remember the fear in Mirka's voice when she told them to go, and Oto would never forget the look of sadness when she realised they would not listen.

And so, despite the warning, Anka and Oto

were still living in the town when the soldiers came.

'Subhi.' Jimmie puts her hand over the pages. 'I've got to go. Sorry.' But even though Jimmie is packing up the Thermos and standing already, I don't want to stop. Not now, when the soldiers are coming. I know from Queeny what happens when soldiers come. 'Wait, just a bit more . . .'

But Jimmie looks at me with that don't argue all over her face.

'Subhi. I don't want it to end. I want this to last.'

I hand back that book without another word. I get it. I don't want my ba's stories to ever end either. 'Good thing you don't know them then,' the duck says quietly. 'They can't end if they never start.' He thinks he's being funny.

'Oh, I almost forgot.' Jimmie holds out another torch, smaller than the one she usually carries. 'We can use these to signal each other. Like Morse code or something.'

I have no idea what Morse code is. The duck says, 'Wait on now! We aren't allowed a torch . . .' But my hand reaches out and takes the torch even though I don't think I really want it. But I guess I didn't want that tattoo at first either.

'I don't know Morse code,' I say, the torch feeling heavy in my hand.

'Oh,' Jimmie says. 'OK. Well, real Morse code uses a whole alphabet so you can write messages and everything. But we'll do our own one. I'll give three quick flashes on my torch to let you know I'm here, and you flash back three times if you're there and it's safe to come in. If I don't see the flash, I won't come.'

My head nods but this seems like a pretty stupid idea, because what if someone sees us?

'Two long flashes means help. That way, if ever you need me, you just flash, OK?'

The thought of that makes me laugh, and now Jimmie looks kind of cross. If she's even a bit like Queeny, I really don't want to make her cross.

'Got it,' I say, and give the torch a practice flash. 'But what if I need help when you're not at the fence?'

Now Jimmie sees the stupid in her thinking and laughs as well. 'Well, it might work further up the hill. I'll try, OK? Watch for me and flash back if you see me.'

As she's turning to go, she says, 'What do you see when a duck bends over?'

'What?'

'Its bum quack.' Then she's gone.

'That wasn't even funny,' the Shakespeare duck says, but it's hard to hear over the sound of my trying to snort back giggles.

After a bit, I see a torch flash over by the fence. I flash back, real fast, then shove the torch under the dirt in case anyone comes.

That torch flashes three more times. Each time moving higher in the dark. I flash back every time. I wonder how far away Jimmie is now. It feels nice, knowing we're talking, even though she's not here.

I wonder if we can learn Morse code for real.

15

All the way up the hill Jimmie turns and flashes the torch. When Subhi flashes back, she lets loose a long howl of happiness into the sky. She wonders if he can hear it from their corner. Or if he's still even at their corner. Or if he's in one of those big tents already. She wonders which tent is his, and how many people he lives with in there.

She wonders what it would be like, only knowing what's inside that fence. Never being able to go exploring. Never swimming in the creek or running down a hill. 'He's probably never even climbed a tree,' she says out loud. Jimmie feels the howl in her throat turn from happy to sad at the unfairness of it all.

How can people be so mean to each other when isn't everyone just the same anyway, and why can't anyone work that out? Jimmie can feel the frustration growing inside her chest until she's just about ready to burst from not being able to do anything about it, and suddenly the whole world seems to get darker, like she is looking through sunglasses.

So when she gets home and sees the phone, the idea just seems to pop into her head. Jonah will never notice it's missing. He's used up all the credit anyway, and when he can't find it he'll probably think that he's lost it himself.

So Jimmie slips the phone into her pocket. Someday she'll show Subhi around for real. But she can still show Subhi everything he wants to see now. She'll show him her house and Raticus and Jonah and Dad and the bike with the bent wheel and her room. And her mum. She'll show him the trees and the river and the termite hills and the ant nests and the bus stops waiting to take him wherever he wants to go.

She'll show him everything he has to look forward to and everything he's going to see. Everything they can share together. Jimmie's never had a friend she wanted to share everything with before.

That night, Jimmie doesn't sleep with her mum's book. Instead, she puts it in her drawer along with the phone. Waiting for Subhi to share it with.

16

Queeny is talking to Eli. She's over by the fence, and even though I know it's stupid, I feel a kind of angry watching him talk with her and not me. Eli tries hard to meet up with me every day, but things are different now that he's in Alpha. Their meals and showers are on at different times and mostly he's always busy with the other men, walking the fences, their heads bent over, talking about things that Eli won't tell me. 'It's nothing. Just boring blabber,' he said when I asked. It's not his fault. He's the one stuck over there. He's the one needing to make friends and keep strong. But mostly now I don't get to talk with Eli. Not for real. And I miss him.

I still haven't told him about Jimmie. I will. I just haven't found the right time, is all. A time when it's just us and Eli is looking at me for real again, like he used to. Some days I get the feeling that Eli isn't really hearing much of what I'm saying any more. Like his head is busy thinking on other things that aren't me.

When I go up to the fence, Queeny shoves something in her pocket. She's rubbish at hiding things.

'Show him,' Eli says. 'Subhi won't tell.' The way he says it makes me feel about ten times bigger than before. I wish more than ever that Eli was back in Family with me.

Queeny looks me hard in the eye. 'You tell even that stupid duck you carry around and I swear, Subhi, I'll rub you in pig fat and set the Jackets' dogs on you, you hear?' The duck squeaks in shock.

Then Queeny pulls out a camera. A real camera. The only cameras I've ever seen were when the newspaper guys came and took a big photo of all of us in here, waiting. I was right at the front and smiling, which Queeny said was stupid because we weren't meant to be happy. I told her I was happy, though, and then she said something so quiet and low that I couldn't make out the words. I didn't ask her to repeat it.

For a while after that, we got a whole lot of stuff from people Outside who saw our picture. They sent us all sorts of things, and each week was an exciting kind of wait to see what would turn up through Security.

But then the newspaper people and their cameras were stopped from visiting and any mail sent to us was returned to the person who sent it, and it was just like those newspaper people had never been.

And now Queeny is here with a camera she's trying to hide.

'It's so people on the Outside know the truth,' Eli says. He's beginning to sound a lot like Queeny. I wonder how many times they've talked when I haven't been around. 'This camera, it sends the photos straight out into the world, right on to people's computers. We don't even have to plug it in. All I have to do is get it into the computer room.'

I've never been in the computer room. Kids aren't allowed. There are only eight computers in there, and the adults are put on a roster so they know when it's their time. I guess that's one good thing about Eli being in Alpha. Now he gets to use the computers.

'It's tricky, though,' Eli says, 'because those Jackets stand right over your back and take notes on all the stuff you try and look up. But I'm doing it, Subhi. I'm doing it. I'm getting the photos out there for everyone to see.'

I smile and nod and say, 'Great,' but both Queeny and Eli know I'm bluffing because the excited goes out of their faces pretty quick.

'You don't get it, Subhi,' Queeny says. 'It's so the Outside will remember us.'

When I don't answer, she shakes her head at me. 'That's why we're all dumped out here in the bum end of nowhere, Subhi. So everyone forgets us. Don't you see? This way, we don't even exist.'

Queeny says that kind of stuff a lot. And she thinks I'm the stupid one.

'But that will change,' Queeny says. There's something about the way she says it, quiet but with her chin sticking out like it does when she isn't going to stand for any argument, that makes me feel all cold inside.

'Soon Subhi, the people out there will remember us. Soon they'll see that living in here isn't living at all. We just need to show them who we are, that we're people, and then they'll remember. This time, they won't forget.' Her eyes zip over to Eli and they give each other a look. I don't know what that look means, and I don't feel ten times taller any more. I feel like I'm not even there at all.

'But if you get caught ... they'll call you troublemakers. They'll put you in Beta—'

Eli laughs and sticks his arm through the fence to give me a shove. 'We won't get caught, little bruda. Don't you worry about that.'

Queeny just shakes her head at me like I'm some vomit she's stepped on with bare feet. 'Some things are worth the risk, Subhi. Don't you see that? When are you ever going to notice what's going on around you? When are you going to grow up?'

Eli turns to Queeny, a quiet hard in his eyes. 'Leave it, Queeny.' And Queeny doesn't say anything else. But neither does Eli. He doesn't even tell her she's wrong.

It doesn't matter that I've been standing there for only a few minutes; I don't want to be at the fence any more. Not when Eli is like this. Not with Queeny going on about that camera. 'Well, I'll see ya,' I say, a lump in my throat. Eli gives me a smile, and the two of them wait for me to walk away before they start back talking again.

Queeny wasn't always like this. She used to be different. It was Queeny who taught me how to read and write and do maths. For a bit, a teacher came and taught everyone. But then the Jackets said it was too expensive and there were too many kids, and that the Outside school had said we could go there instead. Everyone had cheered, thinking on going to an Outside school. But it didn't work out how they said. It never does. The school only had enough spaces for five kids, and in the end those five kids decided they didn't want to go anyway. That was after some of the Outside kids had grouped on them at the school and chased them around with sticks, and the school bus driver wouldn't let them get on the bus wearing flip-flops, and a teacher had made them all miss lunch because they hadn't done their homework.

They didn't bring another teacher back here after that. They just got a Jacket to watch us so we could do dot-to-dots and trace over pages with letters on them and colour in pictures of the flag. But Queeny said that was rubbish and that she knew enough to be a teacher anyhow. She taught a whole bunch of us.

That was when Queeny still looked forward. When she still talked about Someday. That was back when Queeny was still good at playing. We would make up imaginings and Queeny would pretend she was a baddy and chase me over the dirt and catch me and tickle me until the breath got too tight in my chest and I'd snort out snot. Queeny taught me about all sorts. About how to swim and how to ride a donkey and how to climb trees. And even though there was no river or donkey or trees, she'd still make me practise, imagining as best we could. Her favourite was the tree climbing. She told me all about the tree she used to climb back in Burma, and how you just have to take it one step at a time and not look down until you reach the last branch. Then when you do, you can breathe in the brand-new air that is sweet and fresh from the clouds and the best air in the whole world to breathe.

Queeny would make things for me too. Little people from rope and sticks, and plastic-bottle cars and trucks and fences. I'd sort through the stick people and choose one to be our ba. Queeny would say *ói!* and her head would nod yes. 'That's our ba!' Then all of us Stick People would walk out of those fences, like the only reason every one of us was in here was to wait for my ba to come.

For years I didn't get it. That we aren't wanted in this place, or in Burma, or in any other place. I didn't get that we aren't wanted anywhere. For a long time I thought we were just waiting on my ba, is all.

Queeny stopped looking forward a long time ago. 'Why do you need to be able to read, stuck in here for ever?' she said one day. 'Here, we are the dead rats they leave out to stop other rats from coming.' It doesn't really make much sense, though, because no matter how many dead rats the Jackets leave in traps around the place, the living ones come back. If rats don't fall for it, I don't know why people would.

I always told myself that Someday Queeny will remember how to look forward again. And sitting back in the tent I realise that she is. All her talk about soon this and soon that. It's just not the way I thought it would happen. This isn't the Someday I imagined.

17

Nasir died today.

I'm back in our corner, waiting for Jimmie, and all I can think on is Nasir. When Harvey told me, it didn't feel real. That I wouldn't see him again. That I wouldn't sit with him again. It felt more like an imagining. Like when I'm thinking about sailing on the sea or climbing a mountain or riding a bike. My brain can't work out being here without Nasir.

I said that to Harvey.

'Of course it doesn't feel real, kid. You've seen Nasir every day of your life. He's your friend.' Then Harvey held me close, even though he's not supposed to, and whispered in my ear so only I could hear. 'Tonight, you look up at that sky, and there will be a new star there. The brightest star in the sky. That will be Nasir. He's looking out for you, kid.'

Then Harvey went and led a new boy over to Nasir's bed. 'Here you go, son. Make yourself at home. This here's the best Family tent we've got, isn't that right, Subhi?' All I could do was blink at the kid come here on his own, already sleeping in a bed that Nasir just died in. I bet he's a head-whumper. The new ones usually are. I can just tell that that banging will keep us all up all night.

And that boy's got no idea why everyone is staring at him with tears in their eyes.

'Nasir used to sleep there,' I said. 'He died this morning.'

But knowing didn't make the boy feel any better. Instead it made him run outside and pull at the fence and cry. Queeny came and punched my arm. 'Good one,' she spat.

When I curled into Maá and let my tears soak her pillow, Maá didn't even wake up. I moved her arm on to me myself.

I'm sad for Nasir for dying in here, for never getting his Someday. I'm sad for me, too. Nasir understood things that other people don't. Like sometimes, some of the oldies call me Aussie Boy. They say the way I talk sounds just like Harvey, and that even the way I walk is more Australian than Rohingya. They say it to make me feel good, but it doesn't. It just puts more heaviness on my back so that even my footprints are deeper in the dirt, and I whisper the few words of Rohingya that I know, just so my brain doesn't turn to thinking that they are right and that I am only Aussie Boy.

Nasir, he never called me Aussie Boy. Not even once. And now he's dead.

When Jimmie flashes her torch, for a moment I wonder if I shouldn't flash back. Not tonight. But I do, and when Jimmie comes she can tell straight off that something's wrong. She doesn't ask me about it, though. She doesn't even try to joke around. Instead, she just pours us both out a cup of hot chocolate from her Thermos and sits with her back leaning up against mine. We don't even say anything. Not for a long time.

‘Harvey reckons that when someone dies, they turn into a star,’ I say finally.

Jimmie looks up at the sky and points to a star brightening on top of us. ‘Well, if he’s right, that star there looks like a pretty good one.’

It’s true. That star there looks just about perfect.

‘Here, I’ve got something to show you.’ Jimmie reaches into her pocket and pulls out a phone. The screen is cracked up the side and there’s a bit at the top saying EMERGENCY ONLY.

‘Sorry, there’s no credit. In case you wanted to call anyone.’

‘I don’t have his number,’ I say, and we both smile, just a little.

I wipe my eyes, and Jimmie presses at the phone. Suddenly the picture on the phone changes and I’m looking at a white rat.

‘This is Raticus. He’s my pet,’ Jimmie says quietly. She looks at the hurt on my face and must think that I’m thinking it’s bad to have a pet rat, because she says, ‘They’re not dirty or anything. At least, Raticus isn’t. He’s lovely and smart. I’ll bring him in some time.’

‘I killed a rat once,’ I say. ‘A baby. I had to. I didn’t want to. And now all the rats in here hate me.’

Jimmie doesn’t even change the look on her face. Not a bit. ‘Sometimes you have to do things you don’t want to.’ She shrugs. ‘Leave the other rats some chocolate and they’ll know you’re sorry.’

Her finger moves over the screen of the phone and the picture changes again. This time to a house. Just like the ones in magazines, except the garden is full of broken pieces of wood and a rusted car with no wheels, and an old empty bath and a tree right in the middle with beautiful yellow flowers all over.

The picture flips again, and now I'm looking at a bed with a yellow blanket covered in monkeys, and four pillows, all piled on top. The bed looks so big and soft. Queeny was right: real beds and pillows must have feathers in them, because what else could get them that puffed? I try to imagine what it must feel like to sleep on feathers, but I don't know about things that soft. There isn't much soft in here.

Now there is a toilet, which isn't cracked or brown or broken. It's in a room all white with pink flowers on the tiles and a whole roll of toilet paper. Not just six squares, but a whole roll. And no line of people waiting and telling you to get a move on and make it fast. Someday I'll be able to go to the toilet whenever I like and sit for as long as I like and use as much toilet paper as I like, just like Jimmie. Thinking that makes me smile.

The next picture is a man with sad in his eyes and shoulders, and hair as crazy as Jimmie's. 'That's my dad,' Jimmie says, but she doesn't need to. He has the same look about him as Jimmie.

Now is a boy, almost grown to a man, who is sleeping

on a chair, all nested in the pillows, with headphones on and dribble coming out his mouth. I've never worn headphones before, but I've heard about them. It must be strange having music go right into your ears that no one else can hear. A bit like my Night Sea that goes straight into my eyes that no one else can see. Jimmie laughs at the picture of the boy and tells me it's her brother, and that she can't wait to send that picture to all of his friends.

And then the pictures are all outside. I see trees and rivers and rocks and nests and roads and tracks leading to more and more of Outside. Jimmie tells me about each and every one, and tells what we'll do and asks where I'd like to go first. Jimmie takes me all over on that phone.

Then she pulls me in close to her and sticks her head right next to mine. 'Don't look at me – look at the phone, duh. And smile, Subhi!' Her arm holds the phone straight up in the air.

Then she brings the phone down and shows me the two of us, our heads squashed in together and smiling. I don't look anything like I did in the newspaper all that time ago. I look almost grown.

My brain is so full of Jimmie and all her photos of everything Outside that I have forgotten about the book. But Jimmie hasn't. She pulls it out of her pocket.

'Just a little bit,' she whispers, 'please.' Without waiting for an answer, she drops the book in my lap and closes her eyes to listen. I look up at the sky. Nasir's star is shining brighter even than before. I start to read.

The soldiers came at night. By morning, only two people remained in the town. One of them was Oto. He had been knocked on the head by the butt of a rifle and lain unconscious for the rest of the night. The soldiers who passed him by assumed him to be among the dead, and left him to rot or be eaten by wild dogs.

The other person who was neither killed nor taken was Mirka. She had watched the events unfold from her seat in the town square, her fist gripping the Bone Sparrow, her thumb working at the green coin in its centre, fully aware that she could not help a single soul. She waited to be rounded up and killed with the others deemed too old or young or sick to travel. But, for whatever reason, the soldiers did not seem to notice the ancient woman seated calmly on the stone bench where she had spent so many days before. When the last of the soldiers left, Mirka felt the Bone Sparrow burn hot beneath her fingers.

It was Mirka who nursed Oto back to health, and Mirka who told Oto that Anka had been among those taken. It was Mirka who took the Bone Sparrow necklace from around her neck and handed it to Oto. 'The Sparrow will recognise

Anka's soul,' she told him. 'She has rubbed her story deep down into his bones. Perhaps he can help you find each other.

'Follow the hill path to the top of the mountain. There you will find a cave, and inside the cave is my grandson, Iliya. Tell him it is his time for the Bone Sparrow.' Mirka placed the necklace in Oto's palm and patted his cheek fondly. 'Stay with Iliya. Walk your journey to find peace. Perhaps then, you can cheat fate one more time.'

Oto knew of Iliya the healer. Everyone did. It was through his concoctions, brewed inside the cave at the top of the mountain, that many in the town were still alive. Oto turned to ask Mirka what she meant, but Mirka had already gone.

Oto closed his eyes and gripped the Bone Sparrow in his hand. He remembered Anka as a child, rubbing away at the bird as she sat on Mirka's knee, her fierce unseeing eyes matching the sparrow's. Oto wondered how many times Anka's fingers had rubbed at this very place. He felt the wind blow across his face. He knew the same wind would be heading for Anka and their unborn child. He cried his love into the wind and prayed that it would reach Anka's ears. Then he set off up the mountain to find Iliya.

Many miles across the land, the wind blew

over Anka's face as she was marched forward by the rough hands of the soldiers. She lifted a hand to touch her face and felt Oto's tears on her own cheeks. Her ears rang with his call and, despite everything, Anka smiled.

I close my eyes and for a moment, I can feel that wind brushing against my cheek. I think of that wind brushing across the cheeks of Ba. When I open my eyes, Jimmie wraps my fingers around the Bone Sparrow.

'Can you feel it? That's what he's doing. He's keeping the clan safe.'

I can feel a burning so hot in my fingers that I want to pull back, but Jimmie's fingers are held tight around mine and she's smiling. And that hot doesn't feel bad any more. I know now for sure that Queeny was wrong about the sparrow on the bed. It didn't mean death at all. It was bringing a different message. Maybe it was keeping me safe.

Then Jimmie drops my hand and tucks the Bone Sparrow back under her shirt. 'I've gotta go,' she says. 'Come with me?' I think she's joking again until I see the serious on her face. My breath catches, but my head is shaking. Long, slow shakes. 'The duck could come too, you know.' This time she is joking. I think.

'Let me show you, then. In case you change your mind.'

Jimmie takes me by the hand and pulls me up. 'It's

this way,' she whispers. Even though my feet feel heavy and my heart won't stop pounding in my chest, there's nothing in the world that could stop me from following Jimmie.

I thought it was only me and Eli that knew all the squeezeways. I should have known that if anyone else did, it would be Jimmie, for sure. As she pushes her way through and around the tents down behind Hard Road, I can see the Jackets playing cards and drinking, their sticks hanging there on their belts, just waiting.

'You've got to be careful,' I whisper. 'If they see you . . .' I don't know what would happen, but Jimmie doesn't need me to say.

'Don't be silly,' she says. 'I'm just a kid.'

I don't tell her that in here that doesn't matter. Especially when Beaver is on shift, and I know he is because I can hear his laugh. The sound makes me shiver, even though it isn't even a little bit of cold. 'Just watch your back,' I say. 'Everyone needs to watch out. Kid or not.'

'Yeah, yeah. Now, listen,' she says. She pushes my hand on to the fence. 'Every fence has a weak spot. You just got to know where to look, right? This fence, its weak spot is right over here. From this spikey shrub right here, yeah? You walk sixteen steps from here.' She starts walking with me and keeps my hand pushed to the fence under hers as she's counting out those steps. 'And then you feel it. See?'

I don't feel anything. Just the fence. Just the same as every other bit of fence. But then, there it is. Like something in the fence is waiting for me. That wire, it softens under my hand. Jimmie whispers a laugh, seeing my face, my eyes opening wider and my mouth all loose and wobbly, and her hand slaps over her mouth to stop the laughing from making it to the Jackets.

'I'll see ya, Subhi,' Jimmie says, and she gets down on her stomach and lifts the wire just high enough to squeeze herself under. I help her lift it, and when I do, the wind picks up and blows leaves up against the fence. Even though that fence is just wire, somehow that wind feels different coming through that hole.

Jimmie waits a bit, and I realise that I still have her book held tight against my chest. Jimmie holds up the wire for me. When I pass the book through, my hand touches on the dirt outside and sends fire shooting up my wrist, so hot that I have to pull back.

Jimmie, she stays there, holding the book in one hand and the wire in the other. She keeps that wire up, letting the wind feel its way over my face, letting me taste the air on the other side.

I don't know how long we stay like that. It feels like a long time. Like when I put my head under the water. Except this time I don't need to hold my breath. This time I can enjoy the breathing. Enjoy pulling that air deep inside of me. This time the birds don't need to worry.

'And once you're out,' she whispers, 'you head straight towards that old gum almost at the top of the hill. When you reach that, you'll see my house further on. It's the only house with a letter box made out of Lego.'

I nod *ói*.

'OK then,' Jimmie says and lets the wire go. It springs back into the earth, as tight as all the rest of the wire. 'See ya,' she says again, and even though she's turned, her voice shooting away from me and out into the night, her legs don't follow.

'See ya,' I whisper back.

Jimmie waits a bit more then nods. She goes straight up to the perimeter fence, walking in the space between the two fences just like it was any other space to walk in. I've only ever seen Jackets walk in that space between the two fences. The rats don't even go there, in that space.

Just like that, Jimmie pulls herself under the perimeter fence. When she stands up, all the way on the Outside, the wind starts to bellow and blow. For just the tiniest of moments, that wind picks Jimmie right up off the ground, and she's flying in the air, higher and higher until her head brushes against the stars. She laughs and smiles back at me, shining and beautiful. She's up there in those stars, the blackness going on for ever all around her. I can hear the trees calling up to the stars, and the earth whispering out its stories in the wind for everyone to hear.

And then she's back on the ground and padding her way into the dark again before my eyes can even blink from the wondering of it.

But that shining and that smile, I won't ever forget the way they warmed me up. Right down to my very bones.

18

The Night Sea came again last night, lapping at the tent. The duck poked his head out and squealed with the joy of it.

In the morning, there's another treasure, half buried in the sand. It's a photo of a man with earth lines running all over his face, and a smile full of stories. When I look at that photo, that man stares out at me like he sees me as well as I see him. He has cat eyes that are as blue and dark as the night sky right before a storm. I tell that man to let my ba know that I'm still waiting. I haven't forgotten. I'm here.

There's a sick going around the camp. Not just the normal sick where the dust gets into your lungs and tights up your chest, or the scratching rash that goes on your skin all over and makes you even hotter than before, or the ache in your belly that is just there without letting up, no matter if you eat or not. Those kinds of sick are just sorts of camp sicks and they never properly go away. There's a different sick going around. A real sick.

All of us are vomiting and racing to the toilets, and there's not even time to line up or get paper from the Jackets. Six squares wouldn't do much anyhow. The Jackets aren't even trying to stop us either. They just stand back with their white masks on over their mouths and noses so that they don't get sick themselves.

There's a smell and a fug in the air, and even the people who didn't eat the food that poisoned us all are feeling queasy from smelling it. The Jackets try to hose the sickness out on to the other side of the fences, but all that does is make puddles of sickness all over the dirt for everyone to walk through. Useless as teats on a bull. That's something Harvey says about the other Jackets a lot. I said that about Queeny once, but all it got me was a sore arm.

'This is what happens when you lot don't wash your hands properly before dinner,' one of the Jackets told me. That's what they're saying. That it's our fault we're sick. 'You mean *all* of us didn't wash properly?' I asked. He didn't answer but he wouldn't look me in the eyes either. 'And how come it's only the ones who ate the food that are sick?' I said, and then I threw up on his boots.

I haven't seen Eli, but if he was here, I know he'd be raging that it was only a matter of time, because if you keep feeding people food that's off, then sooner or later it's going to make us all sick. I wonder if Eli's saying that over in Alpha. I bet anything that he is.

But it's not just the food poisoning that's making the air smell sick. There's something else, too. A kind of sad angry that's floating all over.

Queeny is sick as well, but she's still sneaking photos with that camera. Photos of us, and the puddles of sick. I wonder if those photos will be able to show the sad angry too. I reckon you can see it when you look at people's faces, but maybe that's just because I know what all these people can look like when they're happy.

Queeny comes up and sits with me, and even though her hands are holding tight on to her stomach and she looks like all her energy has been sucked out of her, she's smiling. 'Eli reckons some of our photos might make the newspaper,' she says quietly.

I'm not sure why that's a good thing.

Queeny looks like she might vomit again. But then she breathes in nice and deep through her nose. 'I'm sick of being a dead rat, Subhi. I'm sick of being invisible. I've had enough. And now, even if only a few people see, it will mean I'm not invisible any more. D'you get it?'

Queeny and I used to watch the new boatloads come through the fence. They were all excited and buzzy going into Delta. Even when they moved into Family, they were still all full of happy, running around like the beetles that fly about the tents. But then something happened, and that happiness whispered up into the air like water on a hot day. Queeny says that's when they understood that no one could see them any more, that this here is just one big cage of invisible people who no one believes are even real.

Sometimes those kids go quiet for a while then get some happy and some chat back. But some of them go quiet and never get anything back at all. And every time that happens I wonder if Someday those kids will find their voices out there somewhere, or if the red dirt in here has sucked dry their throats for good.

I never used to know what Queeny meant when she said that, about being invisible. But then I think of Eli and I think of Nasir, and I think of the different I feel when Jimmie is here. Like someone is really seeing me, really listening. I haven't felt like that before. So when Queeny asks me if I understand, I do. And I wonder if maybe that's how everyone is feeling. I wonder if maybe that's the sad angry sick that's all over the place and funking up the air.

And I wish I didn't understand, because understanding doesn't fix it. Understanding just makes it worse.

It's a good thing the rain came before Jimmie did. That rain washed right through the camp and cleared away all the puddles of vomit. I reckon if everyone had gone out in the rain, it might just have washed away their sad angry sick as well.

But no one went out in that rain except me, and the sad angry around here is just getting worse, filling up the sky with a heavy fog that won't lift.

I'm still thinking on what Queeny said about not being invisible any more when Jimmie flashes me from the fence. I flash her back, a happy tingling my fingers on the torch.

'Hiya,' she says and flops down in the dirt next to me, her shoes in her hand and her bare feet pushing inunder the bush. 'I love feeling the wet dirt in my toes, don't you?'

'Not really,' I say. 'It clays up and sticks my toes together.'

'Hm. Must just be your toes,' she says, then pulls out a piece of paper and a pencil. 'Here, draw a spiral on the paper. I'm gonna tell your future.'

As I'm spiralling, Jimmie pours us each a hot chocolate and says, 'I don't eat octopus, because they can tell the future. And it would be pretty rubbish to tell the future and know you were gonna get eaten, don't you reckon? Do you eat octopus?'

I stop spiralling, my line filling in the paper to the edge, and give Jimmie back her pencil. 'No. I've never eaten octopus either. Well, I don't think so. But usually it's just about impossible to tell what it is we eat, so I guess maybe I could have.' I drink my hot chocolate in one go, letting it burn all the way down.

Jimmie thinks about what I've said for a while, chewing on the end of the pencil. 'You'd know if you'd eaten octopus. Did you know that octopuses have three hearts and blue blood, and two-thirds of their thinking is done in their tentacles? And, if a predator catches hold of a tentacle, the octopus can lose it and grow another one back. They can also find their way through mazes and solve puzzles and they can tell the future.'

From my pocket, the duck says, 'Does she know about ducks? Ask her what she knows about ducks. Does she know that ducks in different countries have different quacks? So a quack in Japan means something totally different to a quack in Hawaii. It's true. Ask any duck.'

'Do you know about ducks?' I ask, then wish I hadn't. Next time, I'm leaving the duck under the pillow.

'Nah, not much. Ducks aren't very interesting. But they taste delicious.' Jimmie licks her lips to prove it. The duck doesn't say anything. I think he's fainted. We didn't know ducks got eaten.

Then Jimmie counts the spirals I've drawn on the paper. 'OK. So that's six. Now on the other side of the paper, you have to write down P.R.I.V.A.T.E. Got that? Alright. Now write down five letters and the numbers zero to eight, plus five things you might want to be when you grow up.'

I write. When I'm done, Jimmie looks at me again. 'So? What jobs did you put down?'

'Um, an artist, a sailor, a poet, a storyteller and a doctor. I don't really want to be a doctor but back in Burma my family were all healers and I couldn't think of anything else.'

'I don't think a storyteller is really a job . . . but whatever. Now, here, give me the pencil.'

Jimmie starts counting through my list and crosses off letters from P.R.I.V.A.T.E. until she's left with the V. She draws a big circle around it.

'What's that mean?' I ask.

Jimmie smiles at me. 'It means you're going to live in a Van,' she says, and then she laughs at the look on my face. I'm really thinking that a van would be pretty great. I just didn't know people could live in them, was all. If you lived in a van, you could drive all over and never have to stop unless you wanted to.

'It's better than living in an Igloo, or an Elevator, or a Tent. Not as good as living in a Palace, though.' She's moved on to crossing off the other letters I wrote until there is only one letter left circled. 'And you're going to live with someone whose name begins with . . .' Her pencil taps at the paper, showing me what letter is left. It's a J. Jimmie says, 'Aw, shucks. How sweet,' and pokes me in the ribs with her pencil. 'Aaaaand you're going to have . . . six kids! Or pets. Either way, that will be one crowded van.'

I'm beginning to feel a bit like the octopus. I don't think I want to know my future.

Jimmie keeps going. 'And it looks like storyteller is a job, because that's what it says you will be. You'd better get some good stories, then.'

I don't tell Jimmie that that's what I've been trying to do ever since I can remember. It's just that the one who has the stories I want isn't here yet, is all.

After that Jimmie looks at me. 'So what did you do today? Anything fun?'

'Um. Queeny worked out that about one-third of our time awake is spent standing in lines. And today that would have been longer because just when I got to the front of the line at breakfast, the Jacket saw I'd forgotten my ID card, so I had to get it and line up again. But then later, I won the Lice Race.'

Jimmie has her chin resting in her hands and her eyes wide open. 'Lice racing? Are you for real? You race your lice?'

'Oh, yeah. Lice are fast. Not as fast as cockroaches. Cockroaches are better at finding their way out of mazes. Anyway, I won with a lice I called Itchy, which is the biggest one I've ever had. Itchy won by so much that one of the girls got angry and squashed him and ruined the game.' That happens with Lice Racing a lot. If I was one of the lice, I don't reckon it would be worth running my hardest.

'Poor Itchy,' Jimmie says.

'And Queeny, she's got a camera and is taking photos, and Eli is sending them out on the computers. She says she wants people to know about living in here. But I don't like it. It makes me feel like there is something bad coming, and there's nothing I can do to stop it.'

Jimmie punches me hard on the arm. 'There. That was the bad coming. Now you can forget about it.'

Even though she's joking around and trying to cheer me up, I still can't get that creeping feel off my shoulders. So when Jimmie pulls out the book, I grab at it, knowing that it will stop my brain spinning over and over and thinking so much. I wonder how Jimmie knew.

Anka gave birth to their son two months early. He appeared in the world quickly and quietly during one of the wildest storms to hit the coast in the history of the country. Anka had never before seen colour; the images in her mind were varying shades of light and dark, accentuated by their heaviness and bulk. But now, curled around her child for the first time, Anka's mind exploded with bright waves of purple, green, blue and red, as colour after colour washed across her, swirling and pulling, embracing her in their brilliance.

And from Anka's mouth erupted a song of pure love.

Through the storm, over the mountains and all the way over the other side of the country, Oto stared at the sky. He would reach the cave soon and deliver the Bone Sparrow to Iliya. For now, he wore the necklace around his own neck, hoping that perhaps the sparrow would grant him the same luck and protection as its true owner, if only for a little while. Despite everything, Oto felt hope. He would listen to Mirka. He would travel wherever Iliya decided. He would cheat fate. With the help of the Bone Sparrow he would once again find Anka.

As Oto started up the mountain, the sky above him blossomed into waves. He watched the great ribbons of colour ripple through the darkness. Oto listened to his wife's love song, glowing in the darkness of the night just as it was glowing in the shadows of her mind. He held tight to the Bone Sparrow hanging from his neck and wondered if he would ever meet his child.

Two days later, when Oto found Iliya busy in his cave, scraping the walls and placing the green mould carefully into bottles, Oto realised that the healer had been waiting for him. That somehow he had known. Oto smiled. Mirka was right. He would find his wife and child. He was sure of it.

Oto handed the Bone Sparrow to Iliya and helped him pack up his medicine into his satchel. They set off before dawn, tracing their way across the mountain. Oto did not know where they were going, and he suspected Iliya didn't either. But the further they travelled, the more clearly they saw how war had ravaged their country.

One day, four weeks after setting off from the cave, the knot of leather holding the Bone Sparrow came loose. It fell from Iliya's neck into the dirt. Oto stopped to pick it up.

It was then that Iliya stepped on the land mine.

The explosion catapulted Oto into the air, stunning him and turning the air still in front of his eyes. By the time he struggled to his feet, Iliya was gone. His severed foot lay precariously on the edge of the cliff, as if carelessly discarded by a passing traveller.

Oto leaned over the cliff face and called for his friend until his voice was hoarse, knowing as he did so that there was no chance that anyone could survive such a fall. As the sun's heat lifted from the land, Oto closed his eyes. He picked up the Bone Sparrow. It was unharmed, except for the coin missing from its centre. Although Oto searched the ground and the nearby brush, he could not find it. With a heavy heart, he put the Bone Sparrow around his own neck and continued along the path.

The story stops and there is a set of directions for how to get to Eva's house, and I wish Jimmie's mum had been more organised with her story-keeping. I think of Oto, walking and walking to find Anka and their bub, but in my head I see my ba. I wonder how long he's been walking. I wonder how much more walking he has to do.

I want to keep reading. To find out how long it takes Oto to find them. If he ever finds them. I don't know if my ba can hear me, but my brain is shouting at him to continue along the path. To just hurry up and get here, because Queeny is sick of being invisible. And I'm sick of waiting.

Jimmie has a kind of squirled-up look on her face. She takes the book from my hands and starts running her fingers over the letters. 'I don't know this bit. Maybe I've just forgotten, but I'd know, wouldn't I? If I'd heard this before?'

I shrug. 'Maybe. Maybe she got distracted in the telling? Or maybe you were just too little.'

'But what if it's not that? What if I'm forgetting? Sometimes . . .' She stops talking and looks up at the stars. She's quiet for so long, I wonder if she forgot that she was even talking. But then she sniffs and looks right at me. 'Sometimes when I close my eyes, I can't even remember what she looks like. You know? Not really. I miss her, Subhi.'

I hold her hand and look up at the stars because I don't know what to say. Even though the stars are the very same ones I've looked up at every night since being born, they look different. I remember Eli telling me that the stars we look at are already dead; we just don't see it yet, is all. That should make me sad but it doesn't. It just makes them more amazing for the strangeness of it.

I give Jimmie's hand a squeeze. 'It doesn't matter what you see. I think it just matters what you feel.'

Then Jimmie reaches into her pocket and pulls out

three pieces of chocolate. 'There's one for each of us and one for the rats.'

We lie back against the bricks and look up at the stars, letting the chocolate melt slowly in our mouths.

I don't even notice that sad angry fog still floating on the air.

19

Maá won't wake up. She's just stopped. Sometimes her eyes open, but she isn't really there. She isn't really seeing. Queeny tries to feed her a bit and gives her water. She tells me to just be quiet. For God's sake would I just shut up and stop asking questions and stop talking and stop. Just stop. Just stop and leave Maá alone and be quiet. Quiet quiet quiet. No one in the tent makes a noise. Not even the babies.

They brought in a doctor today. He's a new one. The doctors in here come and go a lot. Sometimes there's no doctor here for months, and when that happens, you just have to hope on not getting sick. Eli calls it a doctor shortage, just like the food shortages and water shortages. I used to imagine Harvey standing outside filling up a plastic pool with doctors until the sun shrivelled them up to nothing and not a single one was left.

The doctor was here to see Maá. He looked at her and listened and told us to keep her cool and get lots of rest. That's the cure for just about everything around here.

'Useless as teats on a bull,' I said. I said it loud so he heard. But he just looked sad and confused and I wished I hadn't said anything at all.

Then Harvey came in and said to Queeny that they're putting Maá on HRAT Watch too. I don't know why, because Watch is for the people who try to hurt themselves into dying. Like Saleem, who used every bit of money he could find to buy a boat to save his family because bombs kept falling from the sky and killing everyone he knew. He left his country with his whole family but arrived here on his own. He even paid extra because he was promised a good boat with a motor and a roof and life jackets to fit his little girls, but all he was given was a rubber boat with no life jackets and a promise that the seas were good and calm at this time of year. That promise wasn't any good either, and he said that now he'd lost everything he couldn't see why he had to live any more. He was put on HRAT Watch but it didn't do any good. Queeny told me he would be happy now, because at least he would be with his little girls and his wife again.

Mostly it's grown-ups who go on Watch, but sometimes kids do too. Especially kids who have seen so much stuff on their way here that they can't get it out of their heads. 'Coming here is a bit like waking up from a nightmare and then finding out that you aren't awake at all,' Queeny told me one time when we saw a boy try to hurt himself. I tried to tell the boy about the Pebbles of Happy, but he didn't talk English like I do. I gave him the pebble anyway, but it just made him cry big, huge tears that fell without any sound at all.

Maá hasn't tried to hurt herself. She's just tired, is all. So tired that she won't move, or eat, or drink much. But she's not trying to hurt herself. Maá shouldn't be on HRAT Watch. I told Harvey, but he said not to worry.

He told me that the Jackets are just checking on her because she hasn't eaten much or had much to drink and they just wanted to make sure she is OK.

I can't remember the last time Maá was awake. I would have kept count if I'd known, but the last time she was awake I didn't realise she wouldn't be waking up for so long, so I didn't bother remembering.

I can't remember the last time Maá said anything either. Not even an 'Ah, my love' and a kiss good morning. I think the last time was on my birthday when we watched the rain. I think that was it. I love it when Maá talks. Her voice is soft and buttery and honeyed like warm toast. We only get warm toast with butter and honey when there are Visitors, but when we do it makes me think of Maá's voice. Especially when she sings.

When I was little, Maá used to sing all the time. Songs from everywhere she could find them, and all of them happy and bright. Some of them were in Rohingya, and even though I couldn't understand all of the words properly, they were my favourite. One of them was about swimming through the stars and running with the wind. *If we all sing together, our song can light up the dark*.

And those songs, and that singing, it changed the heavy in the air, so that after, we keep that smiling and happy feel for days. But that hasn't happened for a long time. Maá hasn't sung for a long time. I don't know if she even remembers the words.

I say maybe it was a snake bite, making Maá sleep like that. But Queeny says that is just about the dumbest thing she's ever heard, and that if Maá had been bitten by a snake then she would already be dead, and why couldn't I just get out and find somewhere else to be?

There are lots of snakes in here. Sometimes they get confused and wind their way under the fences and into the tents. I don't see why Queeny thinks a snake bite is so stupid. Once we saw a snake with a baby rabbit, eating it whole, right on the other side of the fences. Later Eli told me that the rabbit wouldn't have known. Its eyes weren't even open yet.

Maybe that's the same with Maá. Maybe her eyes are shut so she doesn't have to see everything any more.

Eli is waiting for me over by the fence. He has angry pumping out of him and he won't stop walking up and down that fence, jerking all over. I want to know where his strong walk is, but I don't think I can ask him. Even Eli looks like he's losing bricks.

'They say they're moving a whole lot of us from Alpha. They reckon it's getting too full in here, so we have to go to a Transit Centre. In another country, Subh. Because this country won't have us. Not ever. They're sending us to a country that can't even look after its own people. Where people die of starvation and disease. A country whose people don't want us. They did it before – they put people into the Transit Centre and they all got beaten up and pissed on and told to go back to where they came from. The police were there and didn't even try to stop it. Ishan was told the police even joined in. They can do anything to us there, anything at all. People have been murdered, and no one does anything. No one even tries. We can go Outside there, but we can't work, or go to school, or anything. Even most of the people whose country it is can't get jobs. And the doctors, and the hospitals, they're like the ones back home. They aren't safe. We won't even have enough money to buy food. How are we supposed to live? How are we . . .'

Eli stops walking and kneels down in the dirt, his face squashed up against the fence diamonds so he doesn't even look like Eli at all.

'I'm scared, Subhi. I don't want to go. I'm not a grown-up. I don't want to be one yet.' Eli is crying. Eli, who never shows his scared to anyone.

I kneel down and squash my head up against his through the fence, so our tears are mixing and falling together onto the ants running rings around us. I don't know what to say to make it better.

Just when my whole body feels like tearing in two, and my head is burning with Eli's sadness, a sparrow comes and lands right next to us. It eyes me just like that Bone Sparrow of Jimmie's, and I wonder if it's carrying souls too. Keeping people together. Bringing luck. I think of Oto, walking his way to peace. To freedom. And when that bird looks at me, all of a sudden, I see. I can see how I can help Eli.

I grab his hand through the fence and squeeze it hard, my voice so quiet I can hardly hear it myself. 'Eli, there's a way out. Through the fences. You just have to go sixteen steps and then the fence, and you can go, and—'

Eli shakes his head and cries even harder. 'Go where, Subhi? You're my family. You're all I've got,' Eli wipes his face to get the tears away, but it just leaves red muddy splatches instead. 'We don't know who's going yet. All we know is that fifty of us are due to be moved next week. That's all they'll say. Beaver said fifty are moving and the rest are being sent back to their old countries. But that can't be right. He has to be messing with us. Right?'

I give his fingers a squeeze. 'But, Eli, if they're going to take you, you should . . . There's a girl. She can help. She could look after you or . . . or . . .'

Now Eli's looking at me all strange. 'What girl?'

But before I can answer, he shakes his head again. 'It doesn't matter. I can't bugger off and leave everyone else, can I?'

He's right. Maybe someone else could. But not Eli. Never Eli.

'Just in case, though,' I say. 'You always said, you always told me that you've got to have a Plan B.'

When Eli looks at me this time, he's nodding. I can see that Plan B working its way through his thinking. He breathes in deep, his eyes closed with concentrating, and when he opens his eyes, there isn't even a trace of fear. He says, 'I did say that, didn't I? All right then, Squirt. Tell me, Subhi. About the fence.'

When I tell him, he smiles. 'You're a good man, Subhi. I'm proud to be your friend, little bruda.'

I'm about to tell him more, all about Jimmie and her phone and her pet rat and Oto and Anka and the Bone Sparrow, but then a man from Alpha comes up. He is holding some string and his face is full of scary. I grip Eli's hand so tight that my fingers ache.

Eli, he doesn't look scared at all. He just looks at the man and shakes his head. 'I'm holding off for a bit. I think I've just been given a plan.'

I wonder if the man will get angry, but he doesn't. He just nods at Eli. 'Stay strong, boy.'

He walks away, back into the tent, and Eli turns to me. 'I gotta go. I need to help these guys. But you stay strong too, Subhi.' He squeezes my hand once and follows the man into the tent.

I don't move from the fence. My legs are numb, thinking on what Eli's said. And I can't have been sitting there long, before Eli walks past. He nods when he sees me, but he doesn't smile. He's helping the man walk to the fence edging out to the road. The man has only strong in his eyes, and I can see where he's used that string to stitch his own lips shut. Like that time Queeny cut her arm and had to have the cut sewn tight to let it heal. The man still has the needle in his hand. He nods at all of us, raising his arms like he's just won a race, and lies down on the dirt. Eli unfolds a bedsheet and I can see where the ink of a pen shines through. They've written on the sheet. Eli turns and shows it to all of us gathered at the fence, watching.

WE ARE INNOCENT.

PLEASE HELP US TO BE FREE.

WE CAN'T LIVE WITHOUT HOPE.

When six more men lie down in the dirt, all of their lips stitched so there's no food or water getting in, I feel a shaking that starts in my legs and moves up my whole body, until I'm juddering all over.

Harvey comes up behind me and rubs my arms and says down low in my ear, 'They'll be right, kiddo. It won't last long. Don't you worry about this, now. It will be over in no time.' He gives my arms a squeeze and walks away, not even looking at those men at the fence.

As soon as Harvey has gone, Queeny comes up. She stands right next to me and takes the camera out of her pocket. She gives a whistle, and the men all turn towards her, like they know exactly what she wants. Eli and another man hold the sheet next to them and Queeny takes a picture, and then another. She shoves the camera back into her pocket before a Jacket sees, and Eli hangs the sheet on the fence facing the road.

I think of the pictures on Jimmie's phone and Maá lying in bed and people lined up in the sun with no water and no shade and no food, and my brain can't make sense of any of it. The whole world has gone crazy and the bricks are falling out all over the place.

I can't get the taste of sour out of my mouth.

It's storming. The Night Sea crashes and slams at the tent, making the walls lean over sideways. I can hear Eli's whale thrashing about and bellowing long howls into the wind. Those waves pull themselves through the cracks, trying to reach us, so that all of us are lying wet in our beds, watching our clothes turn to mud puddles on the floor.

Queeny squeezes my hand and says, 'It's just the rain,' but she has to yell it to get over the thunder those waves are making. Even though she says she doesn't believe, I can tell she's scared the Night Sea is coming to wash her away.

No one sleeps. Not even Maá, who is lying in bed, her eyes watching those puddles growing on the floor. She doesn't say anything. Not even when I cosy up into her and brush the hair back from her head and sing her the *tarana* songs she used to sing to me. I don't think she even blinks. The babies are screaming and crying, and their fear eats into all of us.

The Night Sea keeps coming. There is no washing back deep sleep tonight. If this is my ba trying to tell me something, then I've no bloody idea what it is.

I sit awake with everyone else. Waiting for that storm to wash everything clean. For the waves to wash that dust right out of the dirt and leave it still and clear and quiet. Waiting so we can listen to the earth again.

20

It's still and silent when Jimmie gets home from school. Her dad is sleeping upstairs, recovering from his shifts, and Jonah is out with his mates.

It's the third day this week that Jimmie has made it to school. Her teacher told her that if she could get there every day for a week then she would be in the running to win a pair of brand-new footy boots. It almost made forcing Jonah to wake up worth it.

Jimmie sits down at the kitchen table and gets a book from her bag. Her teacher asked if there was anyone at home to help her read it, and she said yes, even though the answer was no. But maybe she didn't need help. Maybe she could do it herself.

But before Jimmie even gets past the first page her eye catches the newspaper lying open on the table, and she stops. There's a photo. Of Subhi's camp. In the background, Jimmie can even see their corner, hidden away behind the bushes. At the front are six men, their lips sewn closed with string, staring right out at the reader. There's a boy holding up a bedsheet next to them. The boy can't be much older than Subhi. Certainly younger than Jonah. Jimmie wonders if she knows who it is. It could be Eli, the boy Subhi told her about. Jimmie remembers what Subhi said, about Queeny and Eli sneaking in the camera to get their pictures out into the world. And Jimmie gets the same feeling that Subhi had. Like something bad is coming and she can't do a thing to stop it. She punches herself in the arm and whispers the same words she said to Subhi. 'There. That was the bad coming. Now you can forget about it.' But it doesn't make a difference.

Jimmie feels a warm hand on her shoulder, and her dad is standing behind her, reading over her shoulder. The feeling pulls back, and Jimmie closes her eyes and breathes in her dad's smell. He looks so tired. He should be sleeping. But Jimmie knows why he got up. He heard her come in.

'Sad, isn't it, love? The way these people are being treated. It isn't right. Hunger strikes, of all things,' he says.

Jimmie feels the cold start in her belly again. 'Do they all have to do that? The hunger strikes?'

'Ah no, love. I guess some of them are making a protest. Best way they can, locked up in there. Just trying to get us to say we hear them. Take notice. They've been in there a long while now, some of them.'

Jimmie wants to ask more. Wants to find out how they can help, so that no one has to sew their lips together. Wants to know why they have been locked up in there for so long. Why no one is listening. Why it is illegal for people to try to save their families. Why it is illegal to want to live. Jimmie wants to know.

But her dad has already slid the paper across the table and is flicking through to the sports pages. When he says, 'Would you look at that? They suspended him for two weeks for just a little shove! What is the world coming to?' Jimmie gets up from the table. She takes her book and goes to her room.

Her mum would have understood. Her mum would have known what to do. But her mum isn't here. Jimmie has never felt so alone.

21

I'm waiting for Jimmie. She hasn't been here for a while now. When I finally see her light flash, I feel how much I've been missing her. There is so much I want to tell her. So much I want her to know. Because just telling Jimmie makes it feel not so bad somehow. Like maybe it really will be OK. Someday.

When Jimmie runs through the dark, over to our corner, and sits herself down, my breath catches in my throat and it's not from the dust getting into my lungs. It's from seeing what Jimmie has done.

Jimmie doesn't just have the book tonight. She doesn't just have the Thermos of hot chocolate. She has an entire feast, all wrapped up in a red backpack, with cups and plates and blue-and-white napkins, and even a rug so the food doesn't go crunchy with bits of dirt. That food looks almost too dreamy and amazing to be real.

It is real, though. And sitting there watching Jimmie get it ready, my tongue aches with just seeing it all sitting there smiling up at me. I nose through all the smells and breathe in all those colours. All the while, in my head I can see those six men who haven't eaten or drunk a thing for three days now, and Maá who barely eats or drinks at all, but not for any reason she's saying, and Queeny with her camera, and Eli with his sheet, and everyone getting more and more buzzy and angry. It takes just about everything in me not to scream up to the moon with all the swirlings of feelings bursting through my body.

All of a sudden I'm blubbering. I try to wipe away the tears and smile at Jimmie, because this is one of the best things in my life so far, and here I am ruining it by crying like a baby.

Jimmie looks at me and nods. 'I know,' she says. 'I hear you.'

My blubbering slows and my eyes mostly dry up, and I wipe my nose on my shirt and I nod back. I know she does.

My hands have already started heaping the food into my mouth, all those tastes that I didn't even know were real, each one different and wonderful, playing on my tongue and filling out my cheeks and rubbing against my teeth. I see now why Eli and Queeny get so angry about the food in here. They know all these flavours and crunches and tongue-twirls exist. I have to stop and breathe through my nose before I choke.

'If you don't slow down, yer gonna spew it up all over the place and that would just be a bloody big waste.' Jimmie spits her food half way out of her mouth to demonstrate then sucks it all right back in again.

There is so much food Jimmie says there's no way we will be able to eat it all, but I say there is no way I'm going to stop. Not until every little crumb has gone, and I don't care if my stomach bursts from the stuffing.

There are pancakes, which are round and hand-size and still warm from being wrapped in a tea-towel. Jimmie spreads cream and jam on top, and when I get it close to my mouth, my nose sucks up its smells and hints at the taste waiting for my tongue. All setting-sun sweet and shell-pool cool mixed together and spread so thick that the jam and cream squish over the sides and drip down on to the rug. I see why Jimmie brought napkins. It wasn't just so she could fold them into a swan shape and pretend we're at a restaurant, like she tells me. I don't know how correct she is in her pretending, but she promises me that someday she'll take me to one so I can see for myself how good her swans are.

She's brought in a coconut so we can drink the milk, which looks more like water than milk and tastes kind of soapy. The coconut is furry and rough, and has a smell of my Night Sea about it.

There are jam tarts and chicken sandwiches that look as good as the photos in the food magazines and taste even better than I'd imagined. There are sausage rolls with an outside that puffs its crumbs into the sky and spreads all over me, and there's a kind of chocolate filled with cream that tastes likes oranges. There's a whole packet of strawberries, and those strawberries are the best thing I've ever tasted. They are the taste of happiness, pure and true.

'You're not supposed to eat the green bit,' Jimmie says, but that green bit is playing on my tongue like nothing I've ever had before, and I'm not spitting out a single flavour.

'My mum used to have a veggie garden. She planted

all these different things and sang to them all to help them grow. Plants love that, you know.' Jimmie stops and I can see the thinking flashing across her face. 'I might start up the veggie garden again. Then I could bring in veggies pulled straight from the dirt. They taste the best of all, with that growing flavour bursting from them right into your mouth.'

I wonder if the Jackets would let us grow some seeds. Maybe just a few. Then everyone in here could have a turn singing to those seeds and tasting that growing flavour on their tongues.

We sit for a long time then, just talking. Jimmie tells me about the footy boots that her school is giving away, and all about rats and how smart they are. 'They get trained to sniff out bombs and stuff. They get paid in bits of avocado and banana. They love being tickled on their stomachs and they even laugh.'

When I tell her about the hunger strike, Jimmie nods. 'I know. I saw it in the paper.'

So Queeny was right. It did get into the paper. But getting into the paper doesn't seem to do much. Not for us. Thinking on that doesn't make me feel bad, though. Not now, anyway. All the food Jimmie's brought in has given me the clearest, strongest, cheering-est feeling I have ever had. I don't think my tongue can ever go back to not knowing. I reckon it will be stuck thinking on those flavours for ever.

When Jimmie stands up to go, all the food turns

to heavy in my gut, knowing that it's over. But Jimmie stops, like she's trying to work out whether to ask me something or not. 'Before I go . . .' Then she pulls out a new book from her bag. It looks like one of the books we used to have in here when the teacher used to come. 'Can you help me read it? I need to practise if I'm gonna learn.'

It seems to me like there is nothing I would like to do more right now. I don't say so, though. I just nod, and Jimmie and I lean back against the bricks, and we go through that book, every page.

'That's a pretty rubbish story,' I say at the end.

'Terrible,' Jimmie agrees.

'But your reading was great,' I add. Jimmie smiles bigger than I've ever seen her do before.

Then she packs everything into her bag, and even though it is scrunched up and sticky and doesn't look a bit like a swan any more, I take one of the napkins and stuff it into the pocket of my trousers. And when we see her mum's book lying there on the picnic rug, we look at it and back at each other, both thinking the very same thing. That it doesn't matter one bit that we had somehow forgotten about the book. It doesn't matter to either of us that we didn't even get a chance to read a single word of the story. It doesn't matter at all.

After Jimmie has gone, after we've flashed goodbye and I'm lying back in bed, my stomach feels all warm and full. And it still feels warm and full when I wake up the next morning.

22

It's almost midnight when Jimmie gets home, but the energy and excitement are still pushing through her. She feels like dancing. She feels like singing. She feels like climbing on to the roof and howling. She can't remember the last time she felt this happy. Really, really happy.

And Jimmie knows it is time. She lowers the ladder leading to the attic and quietly comes up into the dark. There's no need to turn on the lights. Jimmie knows exactly where her mum's things are. She reaches into the box and pulls out her mum's garden gnome, breathing in the smells of her mum drifting up from the bottom of the box. Old Gnome is still wearing the jumper her mum knitted for him when Jimmie was four. Jimmie remembers watching and wondering when she would be able to knit a jumper like that too. Her mum had promised her that one day she'd teach her.

From downstairs, Jimmie hears her dad snoring and Jonah groaning in his sleep. If she tries, she can even imagine her mum sitting up in bed, waiting, just like she used to when Jimmie was little and would climb into the warm between her parents each morning. Jimmie sits there a long time. She closes her eyes and imagines she can hear her mum singing. It's a song they used to sing together to help the veggies grow. 'You have the most beautiful voice,' her mum had said. Jimmie hasn't sung a single note since her mum died, but when she opens her eyes, she realises it is her own voice she has been hearing.

Then her dad lets out a fart and the moment is gone.

But Jimmie can still feel that happiness bubbling inside her. She doesn't put Old Gnome back in the box. Instead she holds him close as she starts back down from the attic. Even when she catches her arm on a piece of sharpened metal sticking out from the ladder, it doesn't bother her. 'Bloody hell!' she grunts, but it doesn't hurt too much. She licks the blood and tells Old Gnome, 'Saliva has great healing powers, you know.' When Old Gnome looks at her and agrees, Jimmie giggles, knowing Subhi would approve.

Jimmie doesn't bother getting into her pyjamas. Instead she kicks off her shoes and climbs under her monkey blanket, nuzzling her face deep into Old Gnome's jumper. Buried beneath the smell of cement and dust and mould is her mum's scent. As strong and beautiful as Jimmie remembers. As she breathes in that smell she realises that the lump and the heaviness in her throat are gone. She wonders when they went away. Tomorrow, she'll ask her dad to get some dirt and some seeds and she'll start that veggie garden going again. Every day she'll sing to those seeds, so they can find their way up through the earth and into the sky.

Jimmie falls asleep with a smile on her face.

23

My brain can't stop thinking about that feast. About the warm full of my stomach that's still there even after a whole day. And when Harvey asks why I've drawn a tattoo of a duck on my arm, I get to laughing so hard that I can't stop and Harvey tells me to get out of the sun because it's making my brain go funny.

I sit next to Maá's bed and draw. This one is for Jimmie. A picture of a girl being born from an egg, and I'm drawing it so that even though Jimmie can't read it yet, she can look at my picture and remember the story for her own self and feel happy.

Some of the oldies ask me to draw them things. Sometimes they ask me to draw them things I haven't ever seen, and then they have to talk and talk until I can see in my head what they have in their rememberings.

Queeny says they only do it so that I shut up for a bit and stop pestering them for more stories. She reckons the only time I'm ever quiet is when I'm being told a story. But Queeny doesn't get it. I need these stories. Everyone else in here has memories to hold on to. Everyone else has things to think on to stop them getting squashed down to nothing. But I don't have memories of anywhere else, and all these days just squish into the same. I need their stories. I need them to make my memories.

Harvey says that drawing down the stories for the oldies is important. He says it's like I'm making the oldies their very own blanket to wrap themselves up in and keep them warm and safe. Even though I'm using bits of paper with stuff on one side and it's too hot here to need a blanket, I get what he means. It doesn't matter that the scraps of memories just get put on scraps of paper to match. Every little scrap joins up to every other little scrap. Every time they tell a story, those words make those joinings-up bigger and louder and stronger, so that soon everyone will see and hear the way the whole world is joined up together by millions of tiny scraps. One day everything will be covered in one gigantic blanket big enough to warm everyone. A blanket full of every story there ever was, and strong enough for every single person to hear.

I tried to explain that to Queeny today. But when Queeny comes into the tent, she's already angry. She slumps down on to the bed and knocks me so the line I'm drawing goes all wonky, but I don't say a word. I'm not stupid. I know a Queeny mood when I see one.

'You bloody well told, didn't you?'

I have no idea what Queeny is talking about. When I don't answer, Queeny grabs my picture. 'You told bloody Harvey, didn't you? You couldn't just keep your stupid big fat mouth shut, could you? And now everything is ruined!'

I grab at the picture. 'I need that.' I keep my voice nice and calm, just like Maá told me to when Queeny gets in one of her moods. 'There's no good in poking snakes, *né*?' That's what Maá used to say.

'Yeah, well, we needed that camera, and now Harvey

has it, all because of you. Harvey said we were lucky it was him who found it because the other Jackets wouldn't just take it and forget. But I know it was you. At least what I'm doing is real,' she hisses, her teeth clenched tight so the words turn angry coming out of her mouth, and she scrunches my drawing on to the ground.

I mean to tell her that the drawing is for one of the oldies, and that for them it is real. But instead, everything comes falling out of my mouth. Everything I wanted to keep for myself.

'This is real. It's not a story. It's a drawing for Jimmie. She's real. She's come in from Outside. You think you're so good, but Jimmie isn't scared of anything. She just walked right in here from the shadows, with a whole book of her maá's and a pet rat called Raticus, and a brother called Jonah, and if she keeps going to school she's going to get a pair of footy boots—'

By the time I'm finished saying everything I didn't want to tell, I'm all out of breath.

From my pocket the duck says, 'She's right. You *do* have a big mouth.'

Queeny isn't even listening. I guess all she can hear are the fireworks in her head. I guess the noise is so fierce that she can't hear any of what I'm saying. She looks at me then and gets down low so she knows I'm listening and understanding. The angry on her face puffs out like smoke clouds from a cigarette and burns as hot as the sun.

'Just shut up! Enough with your bloody stories!' she screams, the words falling like a knife in my ears.

And she's yelling and ripping up my picture for Jimmie. Then she's into the rest of my pictures, ripping them all out in chunks and flinging them out of the tent and into the wind. She's stomping on the ones that have fallen on the ground until they are all ripped and covered in dirt. And as she's yelling and ripping and stomping, the tears are running hard and fast down her face and mixing with the dirt so that soon the pictures are damp and gritty as well.

I stop trying to save them.

Her yelling crashes on my head and bursts through to my ears even with my hands covering them and squeezing so hard I think my head might crack. She's still yelling when I realise I'm banging my head on the ground, whumping just like the new boy, which I haven't done for a long time. When I was smaller I used to whump all the time, trying to thump out my thoughts. That made Maá upset, though, so I had to stop, even though it kind of worked.

There's no use poking snakes, né? So I get up as calm as can be and turn to Queeny. 'I didn't tell Harvey about your stupid camera. I didn't tell anyone. I wouldn't do that to Eli. I wouldn't do that to you either.'

I run out of the tent and walk the fences until my legs stop buzzing and my head stops hurting so much. Somehow I've ended up in Jimmie's and my corner. I close my eyes and pretend that I'm not being yelled at by my only sister, that Maá isn't sleeping all the time, that Eli is back in Family with me, that the men aren't sewing their lips together, that the camp is just the same that it always was. I pretend that the angry sad sick feeling has gone away and everyone is back to being happy and bored instead of angry and sad.

I pretend that Someday everything will be different. Just not today, is all.

From our corner I can look through the branches of the bush and see the squeezeway, and I know behind there is the spikey shrub and the fence where I just have to walk sixteen steps. Just sixteen steps, is all.

I remember how Eli and I used to come here sometimes before Eli grew too tall to fit without those branches poking into him. All those times, we never knew how close we were to getting Outside. I wish Eli was waiting for me by the fence now. But he's not. He's over by the men on their hunger strike. There's eleven of them now with their lips sewn together. One had to be taken to Ford because he passed out and they couldn't get him to wake up. The Jackets cut his lips open and tried to pour water down his throat but he kept choking on it. Harvey told me they were taking him to Ford so they could give him some water and food in a special tube in his arm, was all, and that he'd be fine, I'd see.

I dig my hands down into the dirt, pushing hard against my nails and making them ache so that my brain stops going on about Queeny and Eli and the men and starts on about the ache instead.

Under the bush, the dirt is all soft and a different colour. I guess that must be from where Jimmie sticks her toes under the dirt to feel the earth. Without really thinking on it, my fingers start digging at that soft dirt too. There's something there, though, under that dirt. Something hard. And maybe this digging isn't from Jimmie at all. Maybe there's someone else who uses this corner. Maybe there's someone else who thinks this corner is theirs as much as Jimmie and I reckon it's ours.

I think of my treasures hidden in the tent under Maá's clothes and wonder if maybe I'm finding someone else's treasure. For a moment, I think maybe I should leave it well enough alone. But I don't. I let my fingers grip around that treasure and pull it out from under the bush.

If it is a treasure, it isn't a very good one. Good treasures make people feel good and happy. Good treasures bring stories and memories and imaginings.

This treasure isn't good. This treasure makes my heart stop beating and my breath catch in my throat and my hands start shaking at the stories and imaginings it's telling. This treasure couldn't bring anyone happiness.

It's a knife, so sharp it hurts my eyes just looking at it.

I sit and stare at the knife in the soft dirt until the dinner bell has come and gone and the curfew bell starts up. I take off my shirt and wrap the knife inside.

I wonder whose knife it is. I wonder where they got it. I wonder if Harvey knows. But maybe telling would get someone in trouble. Maybe telling would get someone sent back to where they came from, which is the worst thing that can happen in here. Worse than Beta. Worse than water shortages or food shortages. Worse than sewing your lips together. Worse than staying in here your whole life and never knowing when you'll walk through those fences, if ever.

Queeny says nothing is worse than that. Queeny says that not having a future is the worst thing of all, worse even than being sent back. But I've seen what people do when they're told they are being sent back. Maybe that's what this knife is for.

All I can think is that a treasure like this can only cause trouble.

Later, I'll find the perfect place to bury that knife. A place where no one will accidentally dig in the soft dirt and find it.

If a treasure like that stays lost, then no one can get hurt.

That's what I figure.

24

Jimmie didn't win the footy boots. She missed the last day. Her dad reckons there's a bit of a flu going about. 'One of us was bound to get it, hey, pet?' he said. 'Best not go in to school today, love. I'll bring you up some tea.'

Jimmie doesn't mind being sick, as long as her dad is there to look after her.

When he comes up the stairs in the evening, he's carrying a present, all wrapped up and everything. 'I was saving it for your birthday. But I thought you could do with a bit of cheering up. A sick present, like you used to get when you were little, hey?'

Jimmie smiles. Her eyes feel scratchy and the light feels too bright coming in the window, but she's never too sick for a present. She might even be feeling a bit better already.

Jimmie tears the paper apart. Inside is a blanket. Dark blue with black birds flying across it.

'It reminded me of . . .' Her dad doesn't say it, but Jimmie agrees. It reminds her of the Bone Sparrow too.

'I don't want you to get rid of the other one. I know your mum got you that. You don't even have to use this one. I just thought that maybe you'd be wanting another one now. You're so grown-up now. So here it is. If you want it.'

Jimmie holds the blanket in her arms and lays it across her yellow monkey blanket, the one from when she was six. 'I love it, Dad. Thanks.' And she really does.

'I've got something else to tell you too. I've got a new job, love.' Her dad is smiling, but Jimmie's head starts to pound. She can already feel the tears blurring in her eyes. She doesn't want to move. She can't. They can't leave her mum here. She can't leave Subhi.

'Please don't, Dad.' Her voice feels all hot in her throat. 'I don't want to move again. You promised.'

Her dad laughs and brushes back the hair from her forehead. 'Nah, my lovely. We aren't going anywhere. I've got a job working the grounds at your school. I hope you don't mind. Having your old dad come to school with you every day. At least it means you won't need to bug Jonah to get off his lazy bum to drive you there.'

Jimmie imagines going to school with her dad. Driving with him for forty-five minutes each way, just her and her dad. She can't think of anything she'd like better.

Jimmie snuggles up into him. She wants to stay like this for ever. It doesn't matter that she's sick because her dad is right here with her and that's all she needs.

But her dad moves her slowly off his lap. 'This is my last shift, love. Last couple of days, and then I'll be home for good. Don't worry, Jonah should be here any minute now. He'll look after you. You'll be feeling good as new tomorrow.'

But Jimmie doesn't want Jonah. She wants her dad. She tries to concentrate on this being his last shift. The last time he'll have to leave. But why can't he stay with her? She's sick, isn't she? Why can't he just tell them no?

When her dad leaves, something in Jimmie breaks. Her brain feels too sore and tired to hold on to the good, and she feels like she's falling into a deep dark hole.

'It's his last shift,' she says out loud. 'I'll be OK. Jonah will be home soon, and Dad will be back before I know it.' But her voice is all wobbly and not right. When she pulls her new blanket up around her shoulders, she doesn't feel OK. Not at all. And no matter how hard she tries, Jimmie can't shake the feeling that something bad is going to happen, and her dad won't be here to stop it.

25

Everything is jumpy. There's a fizzing in my body. Every smell is bigger and the sounds are louder and even the light is scratchier.

Maybe this fizzing inside me is catching, because it's not just me that's jumpy. Everyone is. The Runners aren't running packages today because the Jackets look jumpy and fizzing as well. Even their dogs are barking sharper.

There are twenty-four people with their lips sewn shut now, and eighty-seven on hunger strike. Some of the people in Family are on a hunger strike too. I guess Maá is also, just without knowing it. And that zapping has been here all day and won't go away.

I saved the picture for Jimmie. It's dirty from where I wiped the mud away, and Queeny's smudged footprint is right in the middle, but you can still make out the picture of Oto and Anka.

I keep trying to think of my stories, of all the stories I know, trying to quiet the noise buzzing in the back of my head. But that treasure I found keeps poking at my brain, getting me to think on what it means and what I should do about it. Maybe if I can get rid of that knife then everything will go back to normal. Maybe it was never supposed to be found in the first place. I know just the spot, too. A spot where no one will look.

There's a space, behind the toilets and before the wire fence. It's right next to one of the leaky pipes, so no one will look there unless they want to get covered in crap. There's a kind of hole already, leading to under the toilet block, left over from when the toilets were put in. If I can just put the knife there and cover it over with some dirt and maybe a brick as well, then no one will find it. Not ever.

But even after I bury it, even after I'm covered in everyone else's stink from making sure it went right down deep into that hole and is covered over completely, even then, it's still there, in my brain, poking away at me so I can hardly think about anything else.

Eli would know what to do. Eli wouldn't even have paused in his thinking. If he'd been there when I found it, he would have just looked at that knife and said, 'Leave it to me, kiddo. Good job you were around to save the day, hey?' and scrunched up the hair on my head like he always did when I was feeling bad about something.

But Eli's not here. The closest I got was a wave across the compound this morning. He didn't seem to notice that I was waving a 'Come here!' wave instead of a 'Hi, how are you?' wave.

I hope more than anything that Jimmie comes tonight. I reckon that buzzing won't be so loud when Jimmie's here.

And waiting in the dark for Jimmie to come, there's still that sparking in the air, zapping at everyone so I can hardly believe people are actually sleeping.

'A problem shared is a problem halved,' the duck says, which is something Harvey says too. He said it to Queeny once, and she told him if she could shove every one of her problems right up his big fat nose then she would, and never mind about the sharing. Harvey nodded very seriously and sighed and looked as sad as I'd ever seen him look, but then he turned back to me and winked and whispered, 'Teenagers, hey?' I didn't bother telling him that Queeny isn't a teenager yet.

And because I have no one else to tell, I tell the duck about what I found.

'A knife?' the duck says. He doesn't believe me, I can tell. 'How would anyone get a knife in here?'

'Through the packages, I guess. The stuff of kings.'

The duck looks at me again and says, 'Why would a king want a knife?'

'To cut stuff, *né*?'

'Pah,' the duck says.

'What would you know? You're just a stupid duck.' So much for a problem shared. The duck is just making it worse.

That Shakespeare duck looks at me then, and raises one eyebrow the way Maá used to when Queeny and I riled her up with our arguing. 'What would you know? You're just a stupid boy. In some countries in the world, ducks are kings, you know.'

Then we both smile and I tell the duck he's quackers and we smile even more. I take the paper napkin from the picnic out of my pocket, and even though it's nothing more than a scrunched-up paper towel, I can still breathe that picnic deep down inside me and those tastes come back, right on the tip of my tongue. The duck says I'm the quackers one, sniffing at a paper towel, but then he asks for a sniff, and we start up laughing.

We're still snorting when Jimmie comes. That laugh bubbles all the way through me, right over the buzzing and fizzing and fearing, and I feel the same warm and full that I felt after the picnic just on seeing Jimmie in front of me again.

But there's something different about Jimmie tonight. She's holding her torch, but she doesn't flash it first. The way she's walking is all funny too, like she's out of beat. And she doesn't smile when she sees me. She's not wearing her shoes either, and she doesn't even have her Thermos, which is a bummer because my stomach was already looking forward to that burning sweet.

'Hiya, Jimmie,' I say.

Her eyes zip over to me. For a second she looks kind of confused, like she doesn't know who I am. 'Hi,' she says, and her body slumps on to the dirt.

She doesn't say much when I give her the picture. I'm not sure that she really sees it. She closes her eyes and leans against the bush. She doesn't say anything else. She's not even holding her mum's book. She always has her mum's book. But she looks at me all the same and says, 'Well, come on then. Don't you know how to read?' and closes her eyes to listen.

I look down at my hands, the same way I'd do if I was holding a book, and I hear one of Maá's Listen Now stories playing in my head, like it was there all along, just waiting for me to need it. So I pretend to read. Every so often, I glance over at Jimmie, but she has her eyes closed, and her head is nodding, taking that story in.

When I get to the end, the duck claps and says how great the story was and can I tell another now, please, *pleeeeease*?

But Jimmie, she doesn't even make a sound to show she sees that it's finished. She isn't looking at me, or holding my hand, or pulling in her breath sharply at the bits she likes. She's still sitting there with her eyes closed. When the duck says she looks pretty sick, I can feel the hot behind my eyes start to prickle and fall, and I don't know what to do.

Us kids, we look after the babies a lot in here. It's nice. Like adding people to your family. I've looked after so many different babies now that I can tell right away when a baby isn't doing right, even though they can't tell you what's wrong. Sometimes it's not just the babies. Sometimes the kids can't tell you what's wrong either. Sometimes the kids don't know for themselves, and they just get to looking. Staring and not knowing what comes next.

Being in here for ever, I know a sick kid when I see one. And Jimmie isn't right. When I touch her arm, she's all wet and cold and hot all at the same time. She won't look at me. Her eyes blink long and slow, and her toes feel like someone has dunked her in a plastic shell pool full of ice blocks. There's a cut on her arm too, all pussy and swollen and red. 'What happened to your arm?'

Jimmie just shrugs. 'S'nothing. Just a little cut from the ladder,' she says, all thick and hard to hear, and the breath she pulls in is slow, like it's hard just to breathe.

'Did you clean that cut?' I ask quietly. I don't tell her about the germs in case it worries her. But that cut, it doesn't look clean to me. And Jimmie, she's getting hotter and hotter.

'I gotta go,' she says. When I ask her if her dad is home, she looks all confused and then vomits into the dirt. 'He'll be back soon. Two. Only two days,' she says. 'But don't worry, Subhi. Jonah will bring back a chocolate bar.' She half smiles when she says it.

Jimmie starts towards the squeezeway and I follow her to the fence. We count out the steps together.

'Jimmie? Are you sure you're OK?'

Jimmie nods and says, 'Those crocodiles wouldn't bother with me. I'm too small.' If it's a joke, I don't get it at all.

I hold up the wire for Jimmie and she pulls herself through. Then she stands and her whole body shakes with a shiver. From out of her pocket falls her mum's book, splatted on to the dirt. For a moment I'm stuck there, looking at it flapping in the sand like a fish. Jimmie should be picking it up. Jimmie wouldn't ever leave the book there like that. But I know without looking that Jimmie hasn't stopped. That Jimmie hasn't even noticed.

I reckon I could have spent a long time looking at that fish-flapping book and trying not to think. And by the time my body switches off my brain and pulls up the fence so I can reach the book, Jimmie has already slipped under the perimeter fence and disappeared into the dark. All I can hear are her uneven footsteps, way out of beat and losing time.

26

Jimmie can't remember. Her body walks and trips and falls and gets up again and walks and walks. Nothing seems to really matter any more. Every step she takes makes the ground spin and shake. 'Like a giant,' she says. The word GIANT plays over and over in her head, louder each time until she holds her hands over her ears to make it stop.

Suddenly Jimmie is scared. Really scared. She's back home but the door is locked. The phone is inside. Dad and Jonah . . . she needs to phone them. She needs Dad back to stop her feeling so bad. Dad would make her warm again. 'I need help,' she whispers, and no one answers. Jimmie knows that things are bad now.

Where is the key? The window is too high suddenly to jiggle open like normal. The whole house seems bigger, higher, further away. Her legs won't jump, and her hands won't pull her up, and her arm is aching so, so badly that she's crying with the pain.

Maybe, Jimmie thinks, if she just lies down for a bit. Maybe if she just lets herself sleep, just for a little bit, then she'll have enough energy. She blinks and her lids scratch like sandpaper on her eyes.

Jimmie tries to remember if she saw Subhi. If that was real or not. Did he read a story? Her brain moves and mashes things up and the thinking is so hard that it hurts all over.

Jimmie knows what it is to be sick now. To be so sick that nothing in the world seems real. She thinks of her mum, and the Bone Sparrow, and how she never did find out what happened. She wonders where her book is. She needs her book.

Her hand is a torch. No, she's holding a torch. And she needs help. Two long flashes. That means help. Two long flashes. Someone taught her that, but she can't think who. Jimmie concentrates all her energy on pushing the button. On. Wait. Off. On. Wait. Off. She does it three times before the torch rolls from her fingers.

There are no flashes calling back to her. Just dark.

Jimmie doesn't know how long she has been lying there for. How long she has been wishing for water, for Jonah, for Dad, for Mum, for Subhi.

Her eyes close and open, and new stars shine in the dark. She wonders if someone has died.

Jimmie closes her eyes.

27

She'll come back for it. The book. As soon as she sees that she's dropped it. I keep telling myself over and over that I just have to wait, is all, and be patient and stop with my worrying because of course she'll be back.

Then there's that other voice. The one nibbling at the very back of my brain. The one asking me, what if she doesn't? What if she can't? What if she can't, not ever?

I sit down at the fence and finger through the book. All the lists and directions and phone numbers. I try not to think. About anything. I try just to SHUT UP, like Queeny always says. That's when I find it, squished down under a recipe for an egg-free banana bread. The rest of the story. There's enough light coming in from the security lamp to make out the words. My eyes suck them in, and everything else – all the buzzing, all the zapping, all the rest of the world – quiets. I read.

If it hadn't been for Anka's cooking, she was certain that death would have come quickly for both her and her child.

The soldiers were not interested in children, nor in women who could not work. But life was not pleasant for the soldiers either. Food was low and their meagre, tasteless rations did nothing to lift their spirits.

But Anka could change that. She rose one morning, her newborn child strapped to her back, and clicked her way towards the soldiers.

They watched her curiously, this woman who could see without eyes. They watched as Anka went about cultivating a meal that looked more delicious than anything the soldiers could remember having eaten before. As she cooked, she sang a song so full of sadness, it left the men weeping on the ground before her. 'Now eat,' she said, and her food filled the men with warmth and hope and a longing for their families left behind.

After many such meals, the soldiers could no longer stand the daily anguish that awaited them. And so it was that the soldiers released Anka and the rest of their prisoners at a harbour town, and became the first army troop in all of history to desert the army over a bowl of soup.

They were going home to their families.

To thank Anka, they got her a job as a cook on a boat headed to a new land, where they hoped she would be happy and safe, and where they would never more have to listen to her songs. Anka accepted, knowing as she did so that she would never set foot on her homeland again. She just hoped that her songs made it back to Oto's ears. She just hoped that he could follow her songs to find her.

As for Oto, it took many months of working before he could afford to pay for a ticket to a country far enough away to boast peace. Now, finally, as he pushed his way further into the boat, he felt overcome by a crushing sense of desperation. He had allowed the Bone Sparrow to guide him this far. But leaving the country where his love remained could surely not be right. Perhaps when the Bone Sparrow lost its coin, it lost its luck and protection as well.

As the boat left the shore, he felt the hope that had carried him this far vanish into a pit of dread. He would never find Anka. He would never set eyes upon his child. He could not cheat fate.

And then he heard it. The soft mewl of a babe, and a song filled with utter love. Oto pushed his way towards the song, and without being able to see him coming, Anka felt an enormous surge of happiness before being embraced by her husband.

Oto kissed his son and his wife again and again, making up for every lost kiss and stolen embrace. He had never felt happier.

Oto looked down at his son and took the Bone Sparrow necklace from around his own neck. 'May your wings keep you safe and free,' he whispered.

Now I know that I can't wait. That I don't have any choice. That this is something that Jimmie needs to know. She has to know that Oto found Anka, that they are together and OK. That Someday, maybe fate can be cheated, just like Mirka said. That Oto did have the Bone Sparrow's luck, and that now she has its luck, hanging right there around her neck. Because maybe you have to believe in the luck for it to work. Luck is like that. You have to know it is coming to see it when it does. All I've got to do is read her that last bit, and then she'll know and then she'll be right.

I stand up and I look out into that dark, and there it is.

Two long flashes of a torch, all the way up near the top of the hill.

Two long flashes means help.

I don't have time to think. I don't have time to do anything but run. Jimmie is calling for me. Jimmie needs help.

Another torch flashes, and this one is much closer. This one is inside Family and making its way out of the Jackets' Rec Room.

Maybe if I go now – if I'm fast enough.

But I'm not. I'm stuck at that fence, frozen up like I've been standing in that snow where Eli's family went. There isn't just one torch now. There are four. One of them is moving along the fence line, coming straight towards me.

'Move, will you?' the duck squeaks from my pocket, and I move. I run back in between the tents and have just about got back to Family Three when the lights come on. The big, huge searchlights that bright up the whole camp like it's the middle of the day. And I'm caught standing outside the tent with all the lights shining down on me.

All I can think of is that torch flashing up on the hill.

28

I should have gone when I had the chance. I should have been faster. I should never have stopped. If I'd just gone, then Jimmie would be all right. But I didn't, and she isn't, and she's up there on that hill needing me and I can't do a damn thing about it.

It's morning now but those searchlights are still on. Someone forgot to turn them off. Now I bet they'll blow the electricity, which will mean no fans and no fridges for the kitchen and no lights, and pretty soon it will mean the toilets stop working and we'll end up with a river of crap running down between the tents like last time the power went out.

And there's no way to get through that fence. No way to get to Jimmie.

It wasn't because of me that those lights came on last night. It was because of the men in Alpha. It was because of Eli.

When those Jackets came out to do their bed check, they saw that Eli and some of the others had used their beds and blankets and pillows and everything they'd got to shove up against the gates and block themselves in. To block the Jackets out. Now, all of everything in Alpha is piled up against those gates, and the Jackets are patrolling up and down along the fences and not letting any of us near.

About half the men in Alpha are on hunger strike now. Only half. But even so, the Jackets won't let any food or water in. They lay it out right next to the fence, so everyone in there can see the water and food but can't reach out to it.

I keep trying to edge my way to the spikey shrub, to the sixteen steps, to Jimmie, but those Jackets are everywhere. They've brought in even more Jackets than before, and all my edging got me was a bruise the shape of a boot on my back and an ear that won't stop ringing.

Queeny is jumpy and fizzing too, except instead of it making her angrier, she talks to me like she used to, back when I was little. She even said sorry for destroying my pictures and promised me she'd get me a new pad of fresh paper.

I don't care, though. About paper or pictures or any of it. The whole world has turned upside down and I'm stuck here with everything happening and me not doing a thing to put it right. I don't know how.

I walk the fences, Queeny a step behind me. The two of us walk up and down and up and down, and each time I get close enough, I check to see if I can make it through those fences to Jimmie. But those Jackets are like a swarm of bees, buzzing about all over the place.

We're back in front of Family Three when we see the door to Supply is open. There's a big long line of Jackets snaking in to the container. And when the first one comes out, Queeny's grip on my arm gets tight and she pulls me back, away from the Jackets. They're all dressed in their riot gear now. They've got their shields and their helmets and their guns with the rubber bullets that don't kill you but hurt so much that you can't move after.

Even though I don't want to let her pull me, I do. Because Queeny looking out for me starts a soft in my stomach, and I get the feeling that I can shut my eyes and it will all be a dream.

The Jackets in their gear are lining themselves up outside Alpha. Just seeing them coming made a whole bunch of the kids start crying and screaming. I guess for some of these kids, seeing those men all dressed like that brings back memories that are too hard to think about. Sometimes it's good not having memories from Outside.

The fizzing in my body is so loud I can hardly hear anything else now. All I can think is that it's been hours since Jimmie called for help. Hours and hours. And I can't get to her. I can't help. And the Jackets. And Eli. And . . .

Queeny turns to me, her eyes thin and angry, like all that sorry was just pretend. 'You need to get in the tent and stay there. The Jackets with their gear on? They aren't playing any more, Subhi. You need to stay away. You hear me? Just promise me. No matter what you see. No matter what you hear. No matter what happens, you stay in the tent, you got it?'

She's not asking now. She's back to old Queeny, bossing and demanding and not listening to what anyone has to say or think or feel. I can't believe that for a minute there, she made me turn soft with just a couple of words and no good promises.

I think again of Jimmie all hot and sick and calling for help. When Queeny shakes me and tells me again that I'd better listen or else, I only hear my brain screaming, 'What do you care? You've never cared! All you ever do is think about yourself.'

I see the look on her face, like she's been slapped the way Beaver slapped one of the mums that time, right in front of everyone, and everyone just turned away, even Harvey. And I realise I'm not just screaming inside my head. I'm screaming right out loud at Queeny, right to her face so she hears every word. And I don't even care.

Then Harvey is there, rubbing my back and telling me to hush now. He gathers all of us up and waves us into our tents, telling us to stay there. Queeny smiles at me like she's won.

Harvey gives my shoulder a squeeze. 'Don't worry about a thing, kiddo. We'll sort it. It'll all be over in no time.' Then he reaches into his pocket. 'I almost forgot. Here, I got you something.' He pulls out a book. *One Thousand and One Nights*. 'I thought you could read it. To the others in your tent. Might help keep your minds off this, hey?' He gives my arm another squeeze and herds us all in together.

Any other day I'd love a book from Harvey.

The new boy, the one who took Nasir's bed, he's sitting on his bed, looking at me and that book. 'Can you read?' I ask him. He nods. 'Here you go, then. It's for you.' He doesn't smile, but he takes the book and holds it in his hands, just the way I do with my ba's treasures sent on the Night Sea.

But Queeny hasn't won. Because Jimmie needs me. Maybe those Jackets getting their riot gear is a kind of help. It's all everyone in here is talking about. No one is noticing me at all. Like I've up and turned invisible just like Queeny always said I was. Like she'd said we all were. Not even Queeny is looking at what I'm doing. Not since she saw Harvey give me the book. I reckon she thinks all I care about is stories. She doesn't know me at all.

I toe my way to the flap. Harvey is outside talking to one of the other Jackets, but he's not facing my way. It looks like just about all the Jackets are over in the one spot now. There isn't any swarming all over any more. I turn back into the tent to make sure I haven't been spotted, and I see Maá's eyes staring right at me. I wish I could go back and give her a kiss and tell her everything will be all right. But I need to go now. Before someone sees me and stops me. I need to get to Jimmie.

So instead I wave and blow Maá a kiss on my hand. She doesn't even blink.

I leave Family Three and hunch-run along the squeezeways, waiting for a rubber bullet to sting me down. But the Jackets are all outside Alpha. Everyone is watching them strutting up and down that fence in their black boots and black vests and shields and helmets and guns. Everyone is watching the men in Alpha jig from foot to foot waiting on what's happening. Everyone is watching Eli, standing still as can be, right in the middle, and not showing his scared to anyone.

Then I dodge around the last corner and there isn't a Jacket in sight. I'm at the spikey shrub and that wire is just waiting.

One, two, three, four, five, six, seven, eight, nine, ten, eleven, twelve, thirteen, fourteen, fifteen, sixteen steps.

I can feel the wire go soft under my hand. I'm holding Jimmie's book so tight that I reckon I might be leaving my fingerprint marks on its cover. And no one yells at me to stop. No one shoots at me. No one sees me as I push that wire up and squeeze my way through. Then I'm there. In the Space. And still no one has seen me. All the little rats who are too scared to go in the Space watch me, their noses quivering to see what happens next. I tell them that when I get back, I'll tickle their stomachs for them, each and every one, and give them chocolate every chance I get. I tell them I'm sorry for their baby.

I don't run. I walk. Just like Jimmie did. Straight ahead to the perimeter fence. The perimeter fence is higher and has meaner-looking cutting wire on the top, but down here, next to the dirt, the wire is looser even than the first fence.

Then I'm under and those rats are cheering and

clapping their paws together and some are even whistling out their congratulations. Then I'm out. I'm Outside. Now I run.

No one but the rats sees me as I run, faster than I've ever run before, so fast that my brain doesn't even notice that I could go on running and running and running for ever and ever and there wouldn't be a single fence to stop me.

It's not until I've run so far that I can hardly hear the noises of the camp that I stop, coughing up the dirt and the dust and wheezing to get more air into my burning hot lungs. I'm not in the camp any more. For the first time ever, in my whole entire life, I am on dirt that I've never walked on before, breathing in air I've never breathed in before and looking at the world that I've never seen before.

There is nothing and nobody to stop me.

29

I thought it would be harder to find Jimmie. But she was right. It wasn't hard at all. Straight up the hill to the old gum tree. There is the house, the only one with a Lego letterbox. Just like in her photo. With an old, broken bath in the garden waiting to be filled with veggies, and that beautiful tree singing out to us. For a minute my brain stops, just breathing it all in.

But then I see Jimmie. She's just lying there, on the dirt under the window. She is so sick. Her breathing is all fast and sharp, more like hiccups than good, strong breaths, and she needs water. She is burning up even hotter than before.

There is water inside the house. But the door is locked, and so is the window. I see the rock on the ground. It would be perfect for Towers of Rah. It's long and flat and part of my brain is wondering if Jimmie ever played Towers of Rah before, and I'll have to teach her someday because I reckon she'd be good at it. Just not today, is all.

It turns out this rock is pretty good at breaking windows too. I should have moved Jimmie before I threw the rock, because now there is glass all around and I'm worried that she'll get cut again. Jimmie didn't even flinch, though. Not even when the glass smashed and rained down on her legs.

Now I'm in Jimmie's house. I've never been in a house before. Everything is going so slowly and Raticus is just sitting on his wheel, not running, just sitting, and I need everything to be going faster.

But even when I get the water and open the door and try to get Jimmie to drink, the water just spills out of her mouth like she's forgotten how to swallow. I don't know what to do.

Then I see it. Jimmie's phone with the words EMERGENCY ONLY written at the top. Reading those words brings back all the information from the Emergency Folder that I sucked up when I was trying to find something to read. So I do everything the information said to do. I remember to check her airways. I remember to put her in the recovery position, rolled over on her side so she can keep breathing and doesn't swallow her tongue. I remember to call 000.

'You have dialled emergency triple zero. Your call is being connected . . . please wait.'

Don't they know I can't wait? That Jimmie needs help now? Then there is a voice, a real voice of a woman, and she asks if I want police, fire or ambulance. I wonder for a second why anyone would want fire, but I say ambulance and she tells me that I will be connected to the nearest state call centre.

And now there's another voice, and this one's a man and he says, 'Ambulance Emergency, what is your exact location?'

I can't answer. I don't know the exact location. All I know is that Jimmie is sick.

'I don't know.' I can hear the wobble in my voice.

'I need an ambulance. Jimmie is sick and hot and isn't breathing right and I don't know the address or anything, but there isn't anyone else here and it's the house up the hill from the detention centre. You go straight up the hill and head for the big gum and then you'll see the house with a Lego letterbox and a bath in the garden and a tree and—' I talk so fast that I can't even hear the man's voice any more, until he says, 'It's OK, son. We have the address and an ambulance is on the way. Is she conscious? Is she breathing? I need you to roll her on to her side and keep her calm. Can you do that, son?'

Then Jimmie starts calling. She's calling my name. It's no more than a whisper but I hear it.

The man on the phone is still talking, but Jimmie is calling. I can see angry red dots all over her and her eyes keep rolling in her head. I drop the phone and the man sounds all tiny and far away. I talk to Jimmie. I tell her I'm here, and her eyes stop on my face, for just a bit. So I keep talking.

Her lips move and I bend down close to hear what she is saying.

'A story,' she whispers.

I want to tell her that stories don't matter, that she just needs to get better, that nothing else matters, but the man said to keep her calm. And Jimmie said she wants a story. Maybe knowing about the Bone Sparrow's luck is enough to make her better, no matter how sick she is. Maybe knowing will be enough.

So I read her the end of the Bone Sparrow's story. I read, but there is no tingle this time. Just empty words and an ache for something in them to help Jimmie. I put her hand on the Bone Sparrow so she can feel it and know that the luck is dripping into her. But her hand falls off, all heavy and hard.

I keep reading. It doesn't matter that the words aren't a story at all any more but are email addresses and supermarket lists and a reminder to buy red ribbons for the handlebars of a bike for a birthday. I can't tell if Jimmie hears the words or not, but when I read the bit about the ribbons, she smiles, just the smallest bit. Her breathing has slowed down and isn't so hiccupy. I get her to drink a bit more water, and this time she gulps at it. Even though water is still dribbling out the sides, more is going down her throat than it was before.

Now I can hear the ambulance siren and the lights are getting closer and I know that I can't be found here. Not by anyone. Because if they know I can get out, then they'll stop Eli. Eli, he needs a Plan B. He always needs a Plan B.

Jimmie's eyes are closed and her breathing is all crooked, but she doesn't look so scared any more, hearing that ambulance, knowing she'll be OK.

I leave her then, the book resting on her chest so the doctors know that she needs it there to get better, and I squeeze her hand and run into the shadows behind the house.

Her hand stays propped up in the air, like she's still feeling my squeeze.

The ambulance people work fast. They have their bags and their bed and they start on their fixing right away, the lights flashing round and round. They take the book off her chest, but they put it in her hand instead. They know.

They pack her up into the van.

Just as they are about to leave, another car comes and a boy jumps out of it before it is even properly stopped. He screams and calls Jimmie's name and bangs on the side of the ambulance. When he says that he is Jonah, that he is Jimmie's brother, what happened and is she all right? they open the doors and let him in. Before they do I see in his hand. He has a chocolate bar for Jimmie. Just like he promised. And in the back of his car, I can see the handlebars of a bike, glinting silver and bright in the sunlight.

When the lights from the ambulance have disappeared, I can't properly tell if the siren I can hear is the real siren, or just the ringing in my ears, and I've somehow run without noticing, and I'm already half way back to the gum tree. I keep on towards that tree, and when I get there, my legs start wobbling so much that I can't run any more. I let myself sit down on the hill, with my back pushing up against the smooth bark of the tree, and my whole body suddenly turns to mush. I'm shaking and crying and shivering even though I'm not cold or even sick.

And without really meaning to, I start climbing the tree. I remember just what Queeny taught me, back when we were little, when she was telling me all about our home in Burma and the tree they had there. Telling me to take it one step at a time, to look for the next branch along and not stop until I reach the top. And I don't stop. Not until I'm right there on the very last branch.

Queeny was right. The air up here is sweeter and fresher than any air I've ever breathed. Lighter, somehow. I let my legs dangle over the edge of the branch and my arms wrap around the trunk of the tree. The leaves of the gum smell like lemon, and the bark is smooth and soft and cool on my cheek.

From up here I can see the camp. The lights are all still on, and every so often the wind carries a snippet of something. The noise of craziness. I wish Eli hadn't done what he did. I wish he'd just run. Even though I know he had to do it, I still wish he hadn't. I wish it could all go back to being just the way it was before.

I don't want craziness. I don't want any of it.

I look up at the clouds moving across the sky. And something whispers in my ear that right now, right at this very minute, I'm free. I could stay here for ever if I wanted to. I'm Outside. For real, and not just in my imaginings. But as soon as that whisper comes, my chest feels tighter than ever and I don't feel free. I feel scared.

I breathe in that air, trying to get my chest to loosen just a bit, when my nose starts to twitch and I can smell smoke. I look towards the camp again, and I see it.

Flames and smoke eating at the sky. My body lets out a cry without me meaning to.

I can't stay. Not even for a bit.

30

All I can think of is Maá and Queeny and Eli. What if Maá doesn't notice the fire? What if Queeny can't get her to move? And Eli, blocked in with no way out. What if . . .

I tell my brain to stop thinking. To just move and run. Even though my legs have never run like this before, they keep pumping and I can't feel them any more. I feel like I must be flying, they're moving so fast.

Then I'm almost back at the fences. It's like the whole world has turned upside down and been shaken about and there is so much screaming and yelling, and the noise of the craziness is so hot and angry and loud it charges through my brain and even the questions stop.

I stop.

I'm frozen just watching. More and more black angry smoke clouds up from the camp, and I just want to be with Maá and Queeny and Eli, no matter if it means sizzling right up like a sausage along with them.

Once I understand that, my legs take over again. I squeeze through the wire and run through the Space. There aren't any rats any more. Not a single one. I run towards the last fence, waiting for the guns. For the shooting. For the pain. My legs keep running. And the shots never come.

People are running everywhere. Jackets with their shields and helmets and dogs, and people with blood and scared on their faces. No one notices me even though all the other kids must be in the Family tents, staying there no matter what they see or hear, just like Queeny told me to.

All the fences inside are down, pushed over and squashed up in the middle, so there's no Family, no Ford, no Alpha. I wonder if there is Delta and Beta, or if they're down too.

I see the fire reach one of the gas bottles at the back of the kitchens and it explodes so big and loud that it pushes me to the ground. The dirt is in my eyes and mouth and ears and I can't hear anything any more, and a hot something is coming from my ears and when I touch it I see that it is blood.

I get back through the squeezeways, and the sound of the camp is getting louder, and I almost wish for another explosion to make it all quiet again.

There's yelling coming closer. Feet flapping and boots thumping. I fall sideways into the shadows of a tent.

Our corner, Jimmie's and mine, is just in front of me, but it's not a corner any more, just a brick wall and some bushes and a broken-down fence, and I can smell angry and scared and crazy all mixed up together and being pushed about by the wind, which isn't helping anything with its bumping in and out.

And now there is someone. I know who it is just from the way he runs, with his hands straight and pumping in close against his body. I have my mouth open to call out to him. To call out to Eli. Because Eli doesn't have scared. Eli can be Outside for real, climbing those trees and riding his bike and tasting that food, and he wouldn't ever have to stop for anything ever again. Eli just has to use his Plan B.

There is a crash before I can call out and I watch as the outside fences come down. Both of them. Even the perimeter fence. There is no Space now. Just people charging over the broken-down fences and getting caught up in spirals of sharpened wire when they try to jump over.

Eli is running with them. He can jump higher than anyone. He won't get caught on that wire. He's Eli. But he doesn't jump. He stops and spins on the spot so fast that he falls down into the dirt. And then he's up and running again, but now he's running back towards me. Back towards my corner. He's coming for me. To take me with him. But I can't go. Not without Maá. Not without Queeny. And I'm about to call out, to tell him no, that he has to do this on his own, when I see that Eli isn't coming for me at all. He's not even looking my way, and there's a wild in his eyes that I haven't seen before. A scared.

Eli is running towards the bushes. And even though he's too big to hide in them now, I can see he's going to try anyway. Eli wasn't running for me. He was running away. Running away from Beaver. Beaver with his one eye, who hates all of us. Beaver who is chasing him. Eli is scrabbling under those bushes now, trying to get away. Beaver has his black boots and his stick and his helmet and his shield, which he must know he doesn't need because he throws the shield into the dirt so he can grab at Eli better. And he can, and he does, and then Beaver has Eli by the legs and pulls him out of the bushes, out of my corner. Beaver's face is red and glowing with all the hate that is pissing out of him. And I can feel that burning all the way to where I sit, hidden by the shadows of the tent.

And I should be.

And I need to.

And I don't do anything.

Eli fights for all he's worth. Kicking out at Beaver and digging with his fingers under the branches of the bushes where the dirt is soft . . .

Eli is looking for something. Eli won't find that something. He can't. Because someone else took it. Someone who thought they were doing the right thing, but it turned out to be the wrong thing, because maybe now if Eli could find what he is looking for then he might just have a chance against Beaver.

He might just be able to scare Beaver out of doing what he is doing.

But Eli can't, so he doesn't.

I don't move. I don't say anything. I don't do anything.

Beaver pulls Eli out and hits him with his stick. For just a moment, Eli's eyes find mine, and and

And Beaver keeps hitting him until Eli doesn't move any more. Eli doesn't even scream any more. Eli is very,

very still and very, very quiet.

Later I tell myself that I was about to get up. That I was about to push and scream and fight against Beaver with everything in me. That it had all just happened too quickly, is all. Later I tell myself that I was just about to help Eli, who I love as fierce as anyone.

Later I tell myself that the only reason I didn't was because then Harvey was there. Like he'd popped straight out of my wish to save Eli.

Harvey is panting hard and looks at Beaver slowly wiping the blood from his stick on to his trousers. Harvey is as angry as I've ever seen him. He reaches his hand down to Eli's neck and feels for his heart beating. He yells at Beaver and smoothes the hair on Eli's head and rubs his hands over Eli's body and shakes him, saying 'Come on' over and over. His radio crackles. Harvey stands up and starts pushing and pulling Beaver to leave Eli, to *go*. Harvey starts to walk away.

He's going for help. He's going to get a doctor. He's calling for an ambulance, same as I did for Jimmie.

Harvey calls back to Beaver to follow. And Beaver's radio crackles as mad as Harvey's, and for a minute it looks like Beaver is going to go. Like he's going to follow Harvey.

Then I see Eli's hand move. Just a bit. A small flick of his finger, like he's seen me and is waving. Like he's saying hi.

Like he's saying help.

And Beaver sees Eli's hand move.

Harvey turns back too. Harvey sees everything. He calls to Beaver, but Beaver is still watching Eli. Watching his hand.

And then Beaver sees a rock.

I can see now that rocks aren't just good for playing Towers of Rah and Target and breaking windows to get water and phone for help. Rocks are good for terrible things too.

When Beaver picks up that rock, I tell my eyes to shut and my ears to close, but they don't listen.

And then Beaver

And after he

Then Beaver walks away. He walks straight past Harvey, rubbing at that spot where his eye used to be. Harvey is frozen, looking at Eli. Then he follows Beaver.

Harvey walks away.

31

When Eli left his old country, he had to come by truck with his little brother. There were sixty-seven of them, all squished so tight in that truck that their chests ached with the pushing of their breaths.

Even though there wasn't nearly enough air in there for sixty-seven people, and even though they kept asking and begging and pleading the driver for more air, that driver just turned his radio right up and kept going.

When those doors finally opened, Eli, he was the only one left breathing.

Eli said his little brother looked like he was sleeping, all scrunched over with his bum in the air and his legs tucked in and his feet popped out the back like he used to do when he was asleep. Eli said his mum had a photo of his little brother asleep like that from when they were on holiday one time. Eli said when he saw his little brother, just sleeping but for his bluish colour and the dribble of blood coming out from his mouth, he was glad his mum had already been killed by the soldiers, because she wouldn't have to think of his brother being dead every time someone said holiday, or beach, or even just when she saw a kid in a red T-shirt and shorts. Eli told me that his brother dying made his heart bleed so hard that the ache never went away.

Eli was the only one left alive from that truck. I thought that meant he had something important to do.

32

I just have to keep watching Eli's hand, is all. If I watch his hand then I don't have to see his head. Then I don't have to see the rock. If I watch his hand then I can keep thinking that he is going to wave again. To let me know that he is just playing at being so still and . . .

And even though I want to, I don't move out of the shadows. I don't hold Eli and tell him it's OK. That he isn't alone. That I'm here and will do anything for him because he's my brother. I don't tell him I'm sorry. I'm so sorry. My brain screams and my body doesn't move and I watch his hand.

I just have to keep watching until Harvey comes back with help. Harvey will come back any second now. I keep watching, all curled over on my side in the dirt, watching his hand, keeping my eyes on his hand. If I do that, if I just keep watching, then everything will be all right. I just have to keep watching.

I keep watching. I keep waiting.

And then I guess I stop.

The next thing I know, it's hot afternoon and Queeny is there and her head is bleeding but she must be OK because she is screaming for Harvey so loud that it hurts my ears.

'Harvey! He's here! I've got him!' Queeny shakes me and my teeth rattle in my head. I don't want Harvey. I want Eli. I pull on Queeny as hard as I can, bringing her into me, and when she moves, holding me tight and my head on her shoulder, I can see Eli still lying there with people all around. Someone has put a jacket over his head so no one sees what Beaver did.

Harvey is here. My body goes floppy. He picks me up and carries me, and I see all the rest that happened the whole time my brain stopped and closed down. There's no fire now, just a puddle of burnt, and a smell that sours my nose and gets in my mouth and burns my throat. The fences are down, but no one is trying to leave any more. They are just sitting and lying and crying and moaning and the whole world has lost the plot and dropped their load and shy of their bricks and crazy and wrong and rotten.

All through the Visitor Centre, people are hurt on the ground. Some are burnt or bleeding. Some have their hands tied or cuffed behind their backs so their arms are all twisted. Some are calling for help or water. Some are holding their eyes, and I can see the angry on their skin where they have been sprayed with the chilli spray that the Jackets sometimes use when people get too upset and loud. Doctors and ambulances are gathered around and checking people, and the fire truck is still there with its hose out even though there's no fire any more. People are bleeding and crying and calling out, but Harvey pushes me through to the ambulance and tells them to check me over first.

They want to look at Queeny before me. 'It's the ones who are bleeding the most that win in here,' one of the doctors says. But Queeny won't. She says she'll go ahead and bleed all over their goddamn floor and die if they don't check me over right now this instant. Those doctors must deal with people like Queeny a lot, because they look at each other once and don't even try to argue.

'Are you hurt, kid?' the doctor asks. I can't do anything, not even shake my head. The doctor looks at me and says I'm fine, and then Harvey carries me out again. I want to wait with Queeny, but they are already fussing over her head.

Harvey doesn't take me to Family Three. He takes me to the very back of the kitchen. They should be getting ready for dinner by now, but they can't because it's been half destroyed in the fire. There are boxes of food and boxes of water piled up on a table, but no one touches any of them because nobody cares about eating any more.

'What happened, Subhi? Were you there? Did you see? Tell me, Subhi. What did you see?' Harvey's voice gets louder and he squeezes my arms. I look right into his eyes and wish he could pull the words out of my brain because they aren't coming out by themselves.

If this is the real world Queeny keeps telling me about, then I don't want to be part of it. I want to think on a story, but even my stories are gone. Vanished from my head. All I'm left with is an echoing kind of empty, and my stomach feels as though it has been kicked by a truck, and I get what Eli meant about his heart bleeding, because mine is doing that right now. I hurt more than I thought anything could hurt.

'Subhi? What did you see, kid?' Harvey's words push themselves through the hot, wet air, getting heavier and heavier. My brain starts fizzing. I can't make sense of the buzzing and beating in my head. Harvey won't let my eyes look away. Everything is pushing and banging against me. All the treasures, Jimmie, Beaver, the knife, the forest, the gum tree, the fences, Eli. Forever Eli. Harvey grabs my arms and squeezes them tight. The look on his face is madder even than when he looked at Beaver. As mad as a cut snake. Harvey taught me that one too.

But he isn't angry with me. I know because he pulls me into his chest and holds me tight.

Harvey picks me up in his arms and carries me back to Maá.

33

I sleep. I can hear Queeny and Harvey talking over me. For a moment I think I hear Maá, but it can't be. I can't remember the last time Maá talked for real and not just in my memories.

After a while, I stop trying to hear, and I sleep.

The fences are back up. Every one. The Jackets have a book of photos, and they've gone around collecting all the people in the photos, even though the photos aren't good or clear. I know because I saw some when they collected Ilhan from Family Three. Her kids were crying and trying to keep holding on to their maá.

None of them has come back yet. No one knows when they will. If they will. The Jackets say the people they rounded up are the troublemakers. The ones who started the riot.

They had a photo of Eli in their book. I guess they didn't know it was him under the jacket. Or maybe they didn't know it was him in the photo. I knew because, even with the photo all blurred up, I'd know Eli anywhere. In the photo you can see his little brother's red glove in his pocket. He reckoned it gave him good luck and that was why he won Towers of Rah and Target all the time.

I am asleep and remembering.

I'm remembering when I was little, and Maá and me, we'd walk around Family and Maá would point to a bird and say, 'You hear what bird just say?' She used to hear everything. And I would shake my head, and Maá would smile at me and tell me just what she'd heard. Stories the birds carried from one place to the next, or secrets whispered on the wind, or songs the rain played in the warm notes of water falling from the sky. I'm remembering Maá singing the *tarana* songs in Rohingya, and all of us joining in, and Eli listening and drumming his fingers in time, and Queeny getting up and dancing and pulling me to my feet to dance with her. Even the Jackets coming past smiled at us, and one of them went and got his guitar and joined in as well. In my remembering we're singing, '*If we all sing together, our song can light up the dark.*'

I open my eyes. The song is still going. And there is Maá. Awake and beautiful, her eyes smiling at me through the tired, her voice ringing. No one else is in the tent. It's just us. For a moment my breathing stops and my chest is heavier than a million bricks sinking me lower and lower with its pulling. I wonder if maybe I am about to die.

But then my maá pulls me into her arms, and she talks to me in words all mixed up in English and Rohingya, and even though I can't understand the words, I understand the sorry and the promises in them, and I want her to never, ever, ever let me go.

They say it was Eli's fault. They say he started all the craziness. But he was just a kid. He didn't want to be grown yet.

They are saying Eli was on the roof. That he was angry. They are saying he went for Beaver. That he fell. That Beaver tried to save him. They are saying . . .

Harvey doesn't say they are wrong. Harvey doesn't say anything.

My heart won't stop bleeding.

Harvey asks me again if I can talk about it. About what I saw. He asks if I was there when it happened. I don't say anything. I don't say a single word. There are too many words in my head for me to get even a single one out past the sad sticking in my throat. But I make my eyes work themselves all the way up until I'm looking right at Harvey. Right inside him. And he knows. Without me saying a single word, Harvey knows.

Harvey sucks in his breath and pulls me into his chest, and I can smell his skin and clothes and soap, and I reckon he had curry for dinner last night because I can smell that too. 'I tried,' he says. His voice comes out all strangled by his crying. I know he wants me to nod, to tell him I understand, but I can't.

Inside I'm screaming and hearing Eli tell me they're not worth spit and telling me how one day we'll be hot-chocolate chefs.

And I want to see Jimmie. To know if she's OK. To tell her about Eli, about the knife, about Beaver. About

Harvey. To tell her no one knows what happened except me. And Harvey. But he hasn't said and . . . I could tell Jimmie. I could tell her everything.

To see her, is all. I just want to see her.

I look at Harvey. I think of Oto and Anka and Iliya and Ba and Maá and Queeny and Eli and all of us. All of them all that time ago, and all of us now. Just trying to find somewhere to be safe. Just walking our journey to peace. I can hear Queeny's words in my head and now they make sense. I get it now.

'We're the dead rats, Harvey. Just like Queeny said. Left out to rot so no one else bothers to try. There's no keeping safe for us.'

Harvey looks at me like he's never seen me before. But he doesn't say I'm wrong. At last, he gets up and leaves me on my own with the duck.

'It seems to me that you have a simple choice,' the duck says. 'Do nothing or tell what happened.'

I don't want to think about choices any more. Sometimes that duck should just learn to shut up.

'Of course,' he goes on, not paying any attention to my snarling at him, 'if you say what happened, Harvey's done for. Food for the fishes and all that. Because if you say what happened, then they'll have to ask why Harvey didn't say anything straight off. And they'll have to ask why Harvey didn't come back to help Eli. They'll say he is as guilty as Beaver.' Now the duck looks thoughtful and talks as though I'm not even really there. 'Then again, if you don't say anything, no one will know the truth about Eli.' The duck pauses. 'Or maybe your sister is right. Maybe no one cares. Maybe you don't really exist after all.'

I throw the duck so far that I don't even hear the squeak when he hits the ground.

When I wake up it is night. Everyone is asleep. There are more people in here than before because Family Four was destroyed in the fire, and even still, there isn't a single eye blinking.

I can hear something coming. Water galloping towards us. Charging louder and faster. I whisper to Maá, 'Can you hear it? Can you hear the waves, Maá?'

There is a sucking sound and a shadow moves up the walls of the tent. The sound turns into thunder and the wave grows huge and just when I'm starting to think that it's going to wash away our entire camp, the shadow of the wave starts getting smaller and the noise gets softer. It's not thundering any more. I can hear my breathing again and my heart punching against my chest.

Even though the wave has died right down so that it isn't going to wash us away, that Night Sea sneaks in through the zips and the flaps of the tent, puddling on the floor. And it keeps coming. Water fills the tent, like Harvey with the plastic pool. I can feel my cot lifting. The wave keeps coming. All of us float in our beds, rocking back and forth, and the people piled on the floor float on their blankets. No one but me is awake to see.

My hand drops down out of the bed, and I can feel those waves lapping at my fingers. Thousands of tiny fish nibble at the dead skin on my hand. I jump in and push through the water, the fish darting out of the way. I swish through the tent, the water making my trousers and shirt stick to my body and the sand drifting in and out from between my toes.

Outside the tent, the stars are the brightest they've ever been. Thousands of them, lighting up the world. All the creatures in the Night Sea are lined up outside, their heads popping out of the water. Like they've been waiting for me a long time. And I don't know what they want me to do. I don't know what anyone wants me to do. I can't do anything. I didn't do anything. Everything is happening and I didn't do a single damn thing. Even though the water is only up to my waist, I can't breathe properly any more. The heaviness in my chest is pushing harder and harder and I can't get enough air in.

And there he is, the whale, looking just the way Eli said. As big as a country and as beautiful as anything. That water is spinning and turning, but he is as still as can be. He's not singing. He's watching me, his mouth turned upside down and his big eyes shining my face back at me. I touch his nose and feel his breath, hot and wet on my face.

Eli's whale sees inside my head and reads through my memories. A tear, deep and dark red like the Night Sea, swells in the whale's eye and rolls down his cheek and disappears into the water.

'I'm sorry,' I say, over and over, and I can feel my tears falling, deep and dark and as red as the whale's, all the blood from my heart aching out through my eyes and mixing into the waves.

I see every moment I ever had with Eli reflected in the whale's eyes and hear every word we ever spoke, every look, every laugh, echoing in the sound of the waves. My body shakes. I can only say sorry, over and over and over, and those tears keep falling faster and faster, and I wonder if the ache will ever, ever go. There is a fierce inside me, holding on to that ache. Holding it there for ever. So I never, ever forget.

The whale raises his head so his eyes are level with mine, and in the whale's eye I see exactly what I have to do. For Eli. So everyone everywhere can feel that ache, fierce and strong. So no one ever forgets.

Queeny is wrong. We do exist. Eli existed. And now he's gone. And everyone needs to know, to feel that pain tearing at them, even if just for a bit. Just so they know that once there lived a Limbo kid named Eli, and he had something important to do.

I scream out my tears now, and the sea thrashes and the Night Creatures are screeching, whirling and heaving themselves in and out of the water. All the little fish roll on to their backs and pop up to the surface of the sea, their eyes cloudy, their gills still. The whale bellows, a noise so loud it goes right into my head, right down to the very bottom of my skull, and I can feel that bellow echoing in my brain and hurting, hurting, hurting. I close my eyes and the noise gets softer. But not gone. Never gone.

When I open my eyes, the whale is no more than a shadow, and the tide has pulled the sea so far away that I can only hear its waves like a soft whisper in my brain.

But all the way back to the fence, those dead fish are scattered, still and silent. I pick one up and bring it to my lips, and when I kiss it, I can smell the sea, right down deep inside.

34

I wake up. Queeny is there. She looks at me and wipes my hair away from my forehead like she used to when I was little.

When she looks at me, her eyes are so sad it hurts.

'That girl. The one you were making the pictures for. She's real, isn't she?' When I nod, I can see her eyes are watery and red. I turn away.

'I'm sorry, Subhi. I should've listened.' She fidgets around under Maá's bed, looking for something. When she pulls out a book, I feel the pressure on my chest hiccup, and the tightness lets up for just a second.

'It's Ba's,' she says. 'It's his poems. It's the last treasure.' She touches the cover of the book with the very tips of her fingers. The way she says it makes me understand.

My treasures didn't come from the Night Sea at all. Or from my ba. My treasures came from Queeny. Somehow that makes them even more special.

I wonder if Eli knew.

'When old Asiya came to the camp last year, Subhi, she told us Ba was dead. He'd been killed. She knew it was true because she saw him.' Queeny looks at me with eyes so soft I can't remember ever seeing them like that. Not even when I was little. 'I'm sorry, Subhi. But Maá . . . Maá wanted to tell you herself. She kept saying she would, that she just wanted to find the right time. And then she started sleeping more and . . . I guess she just never found the right time.' Queeny shrugs. But I understand.

'All your treasures, they were Ba's. He kept them in his bag. And the book – he took it everywhere with him in his pocket. Everywhere.' She stops. 'Subhi. I know you thought he was coming. But he's not.'

I get it. I guess I've known for a while now that Ba wasn't coming. Not for real.

'It doesn't matter that you didn't meet him,' she says. 'You are so much like him.'

I can feel the tears falling and I don't bother to wipe them away, even though I hate crying in front of Queeny. Because I'm not like him. I'm not like him at all. My ba was strong and brave. He never would have let anyone see his scared. He never would have hidden. My ba would have stood up. My ba would have stopped Beaver. I'm not like him at all.

My head keeps going around and around and I keep seeing Eli, keep seeing his hand—

I'm not like him. But maybe Someday I can be. Maybe today.

Queeny pulls me into her so my head is resting on her shoulder, and she starts to tell me everything there is to know about our ba. When she's telling, the screaming in my head quietens, just that little bit.

I don't know how long we sit there, with Queeny telling me tale after tale of things our ba had done or said or heard or told. She talks until her voice goes all rough and whispery.

All through the telling, I have my eyes shut, and then

suddenly he's there. Right there. My ba. Even though all the pictures of my ba were left behind when Maá and Queeny had to run, even though I never ever saw my ba, not even for a second, I know this is him.

I can tell you every single hair and line on his face, and the big veins on his hands that wrap up his arms like snakes. I can feel the heat and heavy of his body close up to mine and Queeny's. I can smell a smell that is like Harvey and Maá and Eli and the dirt and rain all mixed up together. And I do know him. I've known him all along.

Queeny holds up Ba's book and kisses its cover and puts it back in my hands. 'He would have wanted you to have this,' she says. 'There's even a poem about you in there. It's the very last one.'

She turns to the middle of the book and looks at those words for a long time without saying a single thing. She waits, her eyes pulling at those letters, until the world stops its spinning and the sun stops its shining. When everything ever imagined has paused with expecting, Queeny reads the words, first in Rohingya, then again in English, so I know for sure what they're saying.

When the shadows of fallen stars whisper their truths,
When the wind's kiss echoes in empty fields,
When the spirits of the earth lift to the skies,
You'll be there.
The song of the sea, the soul of the world,

Caressed by the wind,
Scattered in the shadows.
You will see.
And for ever our wings will carry us home, together.

I let the words trickle into my brain, slowly, slowly. And when the poem stops, the rest of the book is blank.

Queeny hugs me then, and it's strong and tight and true.

'I almost forgot to tell you,' she whispers, 'while you were asleep. It was the weirdest thing. All over the camp, there were these hundreds of dead fish. They were just there in the morning after the storm. Harvey says sometimes that can happen during a storm. That a cloud can suck them up from the sea and dump them somewhere else. But for a minute . . .' Queeny stops and her eyes go a bit watery, then she looks at me and whispers, 'for a minute, it made me think of your Night Sea.'

35

Jimmie's back. She's all right. She's here. In the tent. Even though those fences were put back up, even though those Jackets are walking and jingling their keys through the night, even then she still came.

I wake up looking right into her eyes. My lips move but my throat is too tired and worn to make the words come.

She smiles at me. 'I've got another joke for you. Why did the chicken cross the road?'

I shake my head.

'To get to the idiot's house. Knock, knock.'

And even though my voice isn't working right, my lips mouth the words. 'Who's there?'

'The chicken.'

It's not even funny, but I'm laughing, soft and quiet. I say, 'What do you get if you cross a wolf with a chicken?'

'What?'

'Just a wolf. The chicken didn't stand a chance.'

Now Jimmie has her hands on her mouth, quietening her laughing and shaking her head. 'That's terrible.'

'I know.'

'OK then, what side of a chicken has the most feathers?'

I know this one. We end up the two of us saying it at the same time.

'The outside.'

Jimmie smiles at me, and I smile back with everything in me.

Jimmie's fingers wrap around behind her neck and then she has the Bone Sparrow in her hands. She pushes it into my hands and scrunches my fingers around it.

'It's your turn. To wear the sparrow. For now, anyway.' Her face glows with happy. Her arm is covered in a bandage that must have been white before but is rusty from the dirt now.

'Dad's back. For good. So I guess I don't need its luck and protection any more. Jonah said that I almost died so what kind of protection could it be, but I told him that he was wrong. I told him that the Bone Sparrow brought you to me, to save me. Jonah couldn't argue with that. And my dad, he told me that it was just like Mum's stories. Just like Oto and Anka. I didn't even know he knew those stories, but he does. He said he knows other stories too. He said he's going to tell me them all.'

There is so much I want to tell her. But I don't even know if the words make it all the way out of my mouth. There is so much I will tell her. Someday.

'Thanks for saving me and all,' she says. 'Like a superhero. Super Subhi.' Her laugh tinkles in the dark.

I grab her hand and shake my head and whisper, so soft that the sound doesn't even make it to my own ears, 'The sparrow in the house. Queeny was right after all. It did mean death. Eli . . .' But Jimmie hears me. She hears and her eyes go soft and she shakes her head and brings my hand up to her cheek.

'No, Subhi, you're wrong. A sparrow in the house doesn't mean death. It means change. Waking up new and starting again. Subhi, a sparrow in the house is a sign of hope.'

And when my eyes close, it's to the song of Jimmie's smile playing in my head, and the warm sure that something inside me has been made whole.

In the morning, Jimmie is just a dream, floating in my head. But I have the Bone Sparrow in my hand and her whispered words in my ears. Maybe she is a kind of guardian angel after all.

That's when I see the Thermos. Next to the bed, full of hot chocolate, sweet and hot, and thawing me out from the inside.

I find my notebook and pencil and I start to write. The letters flow from deep inside me without even a pause to worry about which way is which and where to put what. And my head fills with memories and stories from so long ago that fences weren't even invented yet. Stories that haven't even happened yet. Stories that the world won't see for years and years. All those stories swirl through my head, but I suck them in and tell them to wait. Because first I have to write the most important story of them all. The story which isn't even a story. The story that has to be told, no matter how hard it is to tell.

36

There are people here. Outside people. They are asking their questions. They have their uniforms and they are taking people one by one into a room. They are asking people about what happened. About all the craziness.

When a woman comes up to me and tells me her name is Sarah and asks if I want to come with her for a chat, I just look at her. My mind is blank and the screaming in my brain is louder than even before.

I see Harvey. He's looking at me.

And already I miss Harvey so much that it hurts.

I look at Sarah. 'Once there lived a Limbo kid named Eli,' I whisper. Sarah bends down close to hear me better. 'And he had something important to do.'

When I look back, there is only sad in Harvey's eyes. A single tear rolls down his cheek. My heart bleeds out even more pain than I thought it could, knowing what I'm doing to Harvey.

But Harvey loves me. He nods, to let me know that it's all right. That he understands.

Then he is gone. And I never see Harvey again.

Not ever.

Oto never did discover what happened to Iliya. The rest of Iliya's story was lost to history, as most existences are.

Iliya hadn't, as Oto assumed, been killed by either the mine or the fall. Rather, he was rescued by villagers and taken to an English doctor volunteering at an aid station. The doctor had travelled to many countries and conversed with many different healers. But never had the doctor seen a concoction as powerful and promising as the one Iliya carried. He realised that this could be what the world was waiting for. Iliya, likewise, realised just how much about healing he still had to learn. So it was without any hesitation that Iliya accepted the doctor's offer to join him on his travels.

Together, they saved many people. And it was in this way that Iliya arrived many years later on the shores of Burma, where he would fall in love with a local Rohingya woman who reminded him somehow of his grandmother Mirka. Perhaps it was her sunburnt nose, or the way she stuck out her chin when she was determined not to lose an argument, or the amazing dark blue of her eyes that looked like the night sky just before a storm.

Despite their meagre existence, Iliya continued to heal those he could, and refused offers of payment of any kind. He became something of a local legend. A famed healer with only one foot. A hero.

His children would go on to become farmers and healers themselves, and their descendants would continue to face greater and greater hardships in a country they had always lived in and whose leaders refused to acknowledge them as people, free to live their lives in happiness and safety.

Burma would become known as Myanmar, and the Rohingya would be told that such a people didn't exist. Many would be killed and tortured and forced to leave. Many would try to escape, searching only for safety. Trying to walk their journey to peace. Many would fear that they had been forgotten by a world that seemed deaf to the cries of those in need, a world in which hope is in short supply.

But Iliya was unaware of all that would come. He would for ever believe that the luck of the Bone Sparrow remained with him, carried perhaps in the greened coin which had once lain in the bird's centre, and which had somehow ended up in his shirt pocket during the blast that had changed his destiny. He had led, he believed, a truly charmed life.

37

'Subhi. Wake up.' Queeny kicks my head with her toes. Maá is up already, at the flap to the tent. Waiting.

'Come on. Hurry.' My heart thumps, but there's no arguing with Queeny.

We tiptoe out, not a word. Queeny and me and Maá, walking our way out into the dark.

'Come on,' Queeny whispers again, her hand reaching out to lead me.

Queeny and Maá have set up a broken post to use as a ladder, and wedged it up next to the container we used as the emergency hospital after the craziness. There's no one in there now, but they've left the container there, just in case it's needed again.

Queeny helps Maá up, then climbs up herself. Then she reaches down her hand and helps pull me up. I can get up myself, but I don't tell her that. I let her pull me, and she smiles.

From up on top of the container, that north wind butts up against us and sends goosebumps up my arms, even in the hot. We can see all the land stretching away from us, on and on for ever and ever.

'Look, Subhi,' Queeny says. She points way out, to where the land ends and the sky begins. 'It's the sea.'

Even though Eli said we can't see them from here, not ever, there's a flickering starting in the sky. Soft green and blue and purple and orange lights are coming in waves, pushing through the darkness, reaching out to us, rippling across the night. Dancing. My chest aches with the bigness of it all, and my body calls out, screaming for something. Those lights are so perfect that I almost can't stand watching them in case that ache gets so big that my whole body will tear apart with wanting.

'Eli, he said not ever . . .'

Maá, she looks at me, those lights dancing across her eyes. 'Not ever can always change.' She holds a letter tight in her hand, the same letter she was given five days ago by Sarah, smiling her biggest smile as she passed it over. Even though I asked Maá what it says, she still won't tell me. Sarah won't either. 'Someday, Subhi,' is all Maá says. She smiles every time she reads it, though.

Queeny shines her face up at those lights. 'Solar flares,' she whispers.

A story runs through me, a whispered memory, every little detail, and I can feel a warm spreading from deep down in my stomach all the way to the very tips of my fingers. 'It's a love song,' I say.

Maá and Queeny don't answer. I wonder if maybe I didn't whisper out loud at all. Maá and Queeny, they're watching the lights, their hands holding each other tight.

Eli was right. Those lights are the most beautiful thing in the world. And Jimmie, she'll be watching too. Watching from her house by the gum tree with the old bath and the Lego letterbox. All of us watching those very same lights, like we're all still together, even though we weren't all of us together at the same time ever. But inside my head we are. Inside my head, Eli is watching those lights too.

I wonder if Harvey is watching. I hope he is.

The Bone Sparrow burns hot around my neck, and I rub at it with my thumb, rubbing my story deep into its bone.

Tomorrow, everything will change. But I'm ready. The Shakespeare duck says it's tough luck if I'm not. He's still sulking after I threw him away. It doesn't matter that I went back for him, and that I spent hours searching for the little bugger. One of the Jackets' dogs had used him as a chew toy for a bit. He's a little worse for wear, and his tail is mostly gnawed off now, but he's still just as chatty. At least now he doesn't squeak.

Sarah talked me through what we're going to do. She says it's as easy as pie – I've just got to tell exactly what I saw and not leave anything out. I asked her how many pies she's ever made, and she said not a single one, but the way she smiled when she said it made me feel OK. Sarah says I just have to be brave, is all. For Eli. For everyone. I told her to tell Harvey I was sorry.

Maá nodded when I told her that I was going with Sarah to tell what I saw. She smiled, even though I could see she was scared and sad. She said I was just like my ba. And she said it in Rohingya.

Sarah made sure I didn't tell anyone what we were going to do, excepting for Maá and Queeny, because all those Jackets are still here and working, even Beaver.

Even Harvey, somewhere. I didn't say a thing, but word must have got around somehow, because when I came into the tent after dinner, there were the rat traps. Every one of them broken, lying on the floor next to my bed. And on my pillow were my shoes. Blue with white laces and the black leaping up the sides. Now they're a perfect fit. I guess I've grown a bit.

From far away I hear a song, beautiful as anything, getting louder and louder and filling my chest with its sound. Queeny, she doesn't seem to notice, but Maá, she leans over. 'You can hear it, *né*?' Her voice is a whisper, so soft my ears almost think I'm imagining. As I lean into Maá, that whale song goes deep inside my head and deep inside my chest, right down to the very middle of my bones. Maá points to the horizon. 'There, in the sea. Under the lights . . .'

And there he is. Eli's whale, as old as the universe and as big as a whole country, singing his song to the moon.

afterword

The Bone Sparrow is an imagined story. However, it is based on an all too true reality. While the characters, events and places described in *The Bone Sparrow* are fictitious, the policies which have put people like Subhi and his family in detention, and the conditions described, are not.

Conditions in detention centres and refugee camps are different all over the world. The conditions I have described in this book have all been taken from reports of life in Australian detention centres. However, the treatment of refugees and people seeking asylum is a global issue.

UNHCR, the United Nations refugee agency, has called on all nations to stop treating asylum seekers like criminals. Across Australia, the UK, USA and Europe, asylum seekers and refugees are routinely detained, fingerprinted and, in some places, numbered.

Hundreds of thousands of asylum seekers and refugees are detained in Europe every year, with EU laws allowing refugees to be locked up for 18 months without a criminal conviction. The conditions of some refugee camps in Europe have been described as diabolical, with appalling hygiene practices, harmful levels of bacteria, and refugees restricted to only one meal a day.

In Australia, asylum seekers and refugees, including children, are locked in detention centres indefinitely, and people arriving in Australia by boat are not allowed to be resettled in Australia, ever.

In the UK, at the Immigration Removal Centres, as in Australian detention centres, there have been protests and hunger strikes over the detention of children; suicides and deaths in custody; and allegations of abuse.

The USA, like Australia, has a policy of mandatory detention. Asylum seekers are detained while their refugee status is reviewed. This can take many months or even years. Asylum seekers and refugees in the USA are often jailed together with criminals, and if they are thought to have committed even a minor offence, can be kept in indefinite detention, sometimes serving even longer sentences than those found guilty of murder.

Meanwhile, desperate people continue to seek safety in countries lucky enough to boast peace. Many do not make it alive. Italy attempted to save the lives of many asylum seekers coming to Europe by boat, by implementing operation Mare Nostrum, a search and rescue operation which is thought to have saved hundreds of thousands of lives. However, other EU nations refused to assist with the high costs of the operation, and it was abandoned after only a year.

It is difficult to imagine what living in conditions such

as these must be like. I hope I have done some justice to the stories of those who have suffered, and those who are still suffering. Since the passing of a new law in the Australian parliament, it is now a criminal offence to disclose the mistreatment of refuges in detention. This deliberate effort to hide the reality of detention makes it harder for people who care to know what is happening, but there is still information available for those wishing to find it. The internet is an invaluable resource, and agencies such as Amnesty International, the Asylum Seeker Resource Centre and UNHCR are good places to start.

Finally, I would like to mention the Rohingya people. Subhi and his family are Rohingya. The Rohingya are an ethnic Muslim minority living in a predominantly Buddhist majority in Myanmar. The United Nations and Amnesty International have declared the Rohingya to be one of the most persecuted people on earth, and a recent investigation by Al Jazeera News suggested that the government of Myanmar is committing genocide in its treatment of the Rohingya. The Rohingya are being hunted into extinction. Governments worldwide are aware of this. They are aware of the plight of the Rohingya. Yet when a boatload full of Rohingya was left stranded in the middle of the sea, no government in the world agreed to help. It has since been suggested that the Rohingya were forced on to that boat and killed if they did not board. Those who did get on the boat were then towed out to sea and left to die. And the world watched. Eventually, after days with no food or water or petrol, the people were rescued by a group of fishermen who showed more compassion and empathy and understanding than all those in power.

I wish this book had never needed to be written. I wish that the circumstances which led me to write this story had never occurred. I wish that we lived in a world where hope and humanity can triumph over the self-serving policies of governments worldwide who are content to imprison those who are simply struggling to survive. Perhaps we will, Someday.

Acknowledgements

Thank you first and foremost to all those who have shared the most difficult moments of your lives so that we may better understand. Without your courage and honesty, this book could never have been written. Thank you also to everyone who has ever had to walk their journey to peace. With you, we are a stronger, more beautiful, wiser and more just society. Thank you for your bravery.

Many thanks also go to my agent, the truly magnificent Claire Wilson, who has the perfect answer to any and every question. You are incredible.

And of course thank you to Helen Thomas, Suzanne O'Sullivan, Hannah Allaman and Emily Meehan for all your combined insights and thoughts along the way. This is an infinitely stronger book because of you. Thanks also to everyone else at Hachette, Orion and Hyperion who have made this book what it is – I couldn't have done it without you.

Thanks also to Rosalind Price, for gifting me your time early on in the manuscript and setting me on the right track – without your advice this manuscript would never have made it further than the scrap paper drawer.

And thank you to Chris, whose place on the

dedication list should have come years ago. In spite of the distance separating us, you have always been there for me and supported me without question. Our couch awaits, always.

Last, but never least, all my love and thanks goes to my wonderful family – Mani, Mischa, Luca and Jugs. You are all my dreams and wishes come true.

about the Author

Zana Fraillon was moved to write *The Bone Sparrow* by the building global refugee crisis. She wanted to remind us all of the people behind the statistics, and to bring the realities of their situation to readers in a way which doesn't shy from the horror, but instead balances it with the power of hope and the strength of the human spirit.

Zana is the author of several other titles for children and lives in Victoria, Australia with her husband and three sons.

You can follow her on Twitter @ZanaFraillon.

Amnesty International UK endorses this book because it upholds our human rights to safety, family and education and shows us what life is like when these are taken away.

Amnesty International is a movement of ordinary people from across the world standing up for humanity and human rights. Our purpose is to protect individuals wherever justice, fairness, freedom and truth are denied.

We all have human rights, no matter who we are or where we live. The Universal Declaration of Human Rights (UDHR) was adopted in 1948, after the horrors of World War II. It was the first document to agree common, global terms for truth, justice and equality. Human rights help us to live lives that are fair and truthful, free from abuse, fear and want and respectful of other people's rights. But they are often abused and we need to stand up for them, for ourselves and for other people.

'Everyone has the right to life, liberty and security of person.' Article 3, UDHR

Now that you've read *The Bone Sparrow*, you may want to think about these questions:

- What does the right to family mean? Who is Subhi's family?
- Who is responsible for this situation? What should they do?
- Why is it important for us to question what we are told?

If you want to stand up for human rights, you can:

- find out how to start a Youth Group in your school or community at www.amnesty.org.uk/youth
- Join the Junior Urgent Action network at www.amnesty.org.uk/jua
- Take action online for individuals at risk around the world at www.amnesty.org.uk/actions

If you are a teacher or librarian, you can use our many free resources for schools at www.amnesty.org.uk/education

Amnesty International UK,
The Human Rights Action Centre, 17-15 New Inn Yard, London EC2A 3EA
Tel: 020 7033 1500
Email: sct@amnesty.org.uk